WE WERE FIFTEEN MINUTES FROM THE BORDER WHEN I FELT THE FIRST HIT—

a laser ack-ack gun from maybe three or four miles behind us.

The second shot came, and it was no ack-ack gun. It was two, no, three stiff volleys from a wing weapon. Our skimmer pitched right, then left. Alloy smelled of burning.

"Mom! I'm scared!"

"Oh, for God's sake, Emily," Sara said.

The next volley came then. This time the skimmer went into a slight dip.

Emily screamed.

I felt like screaming, too.

The Federation ship was hitting us hard and fast. There was a good chance they'd knock us out of the sky before we reached the border.

"Isn't there anything you can do?" Sara Ford shouted.

"Not really. I don't have any military weapons."

"How much farther to the border?" she asked.

"A few miles."

"Then we can make it?"

"I'm not sure

And, as if to   ge
of laser fire hit   tail
didn't simply

DAW is proud to present
these action-packed, hard-hitting
science fiction novels by
DANIEL RANSOM:

THE FUGITIVE STARS

ZONE SOLDIERS

ZONE SOLDIERS

Daniel Ransom

D A W   B O O K S ,   I N C .
DONALD   A.   WOLLHEIM,   FOUNDER
375 Hudson Street. New York, NY 10014

ELIZABETH R. WOLLHEIM
SHEILA E. GILBERT
PUBLISHERS

First Printing, December 1996

1 2 3 4 5 6 7 8 9

DAW TRADEMARK REGISTERED
U.S. PAT. OFF. AND FOREIGN COUNTRIES
—MARCA REGISTRADA
HECHO EN U.S.A.

PRINTED IN THE U.S.A.

To my good friend, Marlys Brunsting,
for all sorts of reasons, but mostly
for making me look a lot better
than I deserve.

PART ONE

1

They got me pretty good, I'll have to give them that.

The first thing they got was my brand-new D-4 jet turbo, a skimmer with a double capacity cargo load.

The second thing they got was my body—broken arm, broken leg, cracked rib, minor concussion, two black eyes, and a faint humming noise in my left ear that still hasn't quite gone away.

The third thing they got was my pride.

I've been flying skimmers over the Zone for the past fourteen years, and this was the first time I'd ever been shot down.

I'd been lucky, of course, though I liked to think it was also my skill as a pilot that kept me from getting knocked out of the sky.

In all, I was in the hospital three-and-a-half weeks.

There were some complications with my right leg, complications that meant I'd have a slight limp for the rest of my life.

I looked at myself in the mirror a lot and realized that I was no longer a boy. That's a funny thing; you can go along still feeling like a kid all through your twenties and maybe even your thirties, and then something happens to you and you're never able to feel like a kid again.

I guess getting shot down took all the kid out of me.

I even wondered about flying over the Zone again.

A lot of pilots quit when they get shot down. If they're lucky enough to survive, that is.

A good number of them die in the crash.

And a lot of them get taken captive by the various kinds of tribes that roam the Zone.

You've seen the holos. I don't have to tell you about some of the mutant gangs down there. . . .

You can get pretty crazy lying there in the hospital, and I guess I probably did.

At least ten times, I resolved that I'd give up flying the Zone and would go out and get myself a nice, sensible job.

But you know what?

It was that thing about not being a kid any more.

It was just too late to do anything else at my age.

Like it or not, I was a Zoner.

And I'd probably always *be* a Zoner until the day I died.

And the way things were going, maybe that wasn't real far away.

Maybe that wasn't real far away at all.

2

He couldn't have been much more than twenty or so.

They'd ripped off his jacket and shirt and cut off both of his good arms. Oddly enough, they'd left intact the little flipperlike appendage that jutted out several inches from a point just above his ribs on the left side, the one that had been his curse and made him an Undesirable.

Then they'd hanged him.

There wasn't anything special about this, of course, an Undesirable sneaking over from the Zone and trying to make a life for himself in the Federation.

Undesirables sneak over all the time. They also get found out all the time by their neighbors or coworkers. And then they get lynched. As one recent candidate for Federation President said: "Lynching Undesirables is not only legal, it is an act of patriotism." His words inspired at least a half-dozen teenage gangs to go out and lynch, in their fervor, completely innocent people.

Teenagers did most of the lynching. They'd probably done this one.

By now, I should have been used to it. I'd grown up in the Federation—that sprawl of states that was roughly the same configuration of land that had made up the original thirteen colonies—but somehow the ugliness of it still got to me. Maybe some of the Federation lands along the West Coast were nicer, but if so I hadn't noticed it on the cargo runs I'd made.

Sweet May morning, neighborhood kids running and jumping and giggling, robins and jays and cardinals singing their asses off, young pretty mothers pushing strollers up and down the sunny sidewalks—and a neck-broke hacked-and-slashed young man hanging from the branch of an oak.

I could have taken my landcar but decided to walk. Too beautiful a morning for landcars. I still limped a little from the crash, but the pleasure of the outdoors was worth the slight pain.

I went three blocks before I became aware of him.

Tailing people is not easy. In adventure holos, all you have to do is put yourself about half a block behind the person you're tailing, and then simply keep pace with him.

In reality, you have to know when to slow down, when to speed up, and you have to be ready to look perfectly innocent if the person you're tailing should suddenly turn around and see you.

We came to a busy intersection, and that's when I spotted him.

I crossed all right, but he got stuck behind a long stream of rushing landcars. He had to hurry to catch up to me because I'd taken an abrupt right and had fallen out of his view.

He overdid it.

He came around the corner a little too fast, enough that I sensed him, and turned around and looked at him, and knew him immediately for what he was.

He tried looking innocent, but it was no good.

He wore the same kind of dark blue jumpsuit that all of us citizens did, the one with the Federation starburst on the breast pocket. He was gangly and red-haired and looked altogether too young to be following a battered and somewhat bitter forty-year-old like me, especially one who'd been forced to kill a couple of people without feeling any noticeable guilt.

I walked on.

I had an appointment at the skimmer shop, and I meant to keep it. If my friend wanted to join me, fine.

Intersections continued to give him trouble. There were four more before I reached the skimmer shop, and my new buddy lost me at every one of them. He'd hang back till too late, apparently afraid that he'd bump into me if he moved any faster, and then landcars would come along and block his way.

Mostly, I forgot about him, and concentrated

on the sweet faces of the little kids, and the kittens in the grass playing with string and babies and dandelions, and the friendly people in the driveways shining up their landcars.

The skimmer shop is one of those masculine provinces composed of certain smells—grease, dust, exhaust—and certain sounds, mostly derisive laughter and cursing. There's also a lot of engine noise, and the creak of hoists lifting skimmers high for examination, and the clank of tools hitting the concrete floor. There's also the hum of robots rushing about on their squatty little legs. They do most of the computer work.

Most of the skimmers repaired here run to the citizen who has saved his credits and bought himself the air skimmer he always dreamed of. On weekends, he gets to sit in the cockpit, take the skimmer up to 35,000 feet, and play hero. Never daring to leave Federation airspace and drift over into the Zone. That's where weekend heroes get their asses shot off, the Zone. You never know who's down on the ground with surface-to-air missiles. About a hundred weekend heroes a year get killed this way. A lot of them take their families with them.

There's a large attached garage to the skimmer shop main building, though, where a special type of skimmer is worked on.

This is the type I fly. These skimmers are twice the size of the family model, and they're loaded with a variety of weapons, including streakers, which are essentially air-to-surface missiles. The cockpit seats three, there is ample storage room in back, and the wings are so well-fortified that only a missile can break them up. There is no small-arms fire that can do more than dent them. The big commercial craft can fly high enough and fast enough, and respond powerfully enough, so that the Zone gunners never bother them. But pilots like me . . .

This is the type of skimmer you fly when you're a Zone pilot, a man or woman who makes a living flying from coast to coast. More than three-quarters of Middle America makes up the Zone. In a skimmer the trip takes seven hours, five of those hours over the Zone proper. A lot can, and does, go wrong.

I walked back to the large attached garage and had a look at the used skimmer I'd bought, the one Marvin was bringing up to combat readiness.

Marvin came up.

"You're gonna kick some ass in this puppy, Duvall," he said, patting my skimmer on the wing. "The guns we installed are mothers, believe me." He winked at me.

Marvin is bald, buck-toothed, and a winker. He underscores about every fifth or sixth remark with a wink.

He pawed grease off on his black work clothes.

"It'll be ready to go in a couple of days."

"How much?"

"Afraid it's a little more than I told you it would be." He winked. "But it's between friends, right?"

"How much?"

I usually jack up Marvin's estimations by about thirty percent, which usually puts me about ten percent under the actual charges. It used to piss me off. Now I realize it's just the way a lot of small businesses have been trained to operate. Lowball your bid and then pray to God your customers will come back after you hit them with the inflated price.

He told me the price.

I didn't argue.

When you're flying over the Zone, and the ground fire is suddenly coming in your direction, you don't think about how much your skimmer mechanic overcharged you. You think about what a good job he did making your craft tight, fast, and safe.

He walked me out to the front of the shop.

I looked for the red-haired kid who'd been following me. I saw him down at the far end of the block. He was sitting on a bench that people waiting for airbuses used. He was reading a magazine and paying me elaborate inattention.

"Noticed you were still limping," Marvin said. "From getting shot down?"

"Yeah. Probably be with me the rest of my life."

"Chicks probably dig it."

"Oh?"

"Vulnerability. The old lady tells me that turns chicks on."

"Vulnerable like you, huh, Marvin?"

He winked. "Old Marvin's got all the vulnerability he needs right in his pants, if you catch my drift."

"I catch your drift."

The black landcar came around the far corner without slowing down until it reached the airbus bench.

Redhair looked up from his magazine, but too late.

By the time he was rising from the bench, two men built like sumo wrestlers burst from the landcar with surprising speed and grabbed him.

One of the men put a fist directly on Redhair's jaw, while the other sent a fist deep into Redhair's belly.

The kid folded in half.

They dragged him into the long black landcar with the black windows, pitching him into the back seat. They got in after him.

The landcar started roaring down the street toward us and then angled upward abruptly.

"I'll be damned," Marvin said. "It's one of those new babies."

"Yeah," I said.

Last year, the convertible, as it had come to be called, was put on the market.

You could use it as a landcar or a skimmer.

The big black car was now several hundred feet in the air, and going higher.

"Wonder who the hell that kid was," Marvin said.

"That's what I wonder."

"Maybe he was an Undesirable."

"Maybe."

"My oldest boy bagged one the other night."

"An Undesirable?"

"Uh-huh. His first one."

I didn't congratulate him. I simply nodded, noting what he'd said.

Marvin didn't pick up on my displeasure.

"Saw this teenage girl sittin' in this little park real late at night, so him and his two pals go over, and damned if she doesn't turn out to be wearing gloves. You know how hot it was the other night."

"Yeah."

"So, anyway, she's got these gloves on, so of course right away my kid and his pals are suspicious. They tell her to take her gloves off, but she won't. She offers to do 'em up, you know what I mean, go down on them and everything, but they've already figured out what she is, and they sure don't want to have sex with anybody like her. So my kid grabs her one arm and rips her glove off and guess what? Seven fingers. I mean, personally, I see seven fingers like that, I'd blow lunch. I hate that mutie shit. But my kid keeps his cool and informs her that as a citizen he has the duty to kill her. He did it with his belt. Used it like a lynch rope, I mean. After they killed her, he ran home and got the holo camera and took some shots of her hangin' from the tree, and man, the old lady and I're so proud of him, you just can't believe it." He winked. "Some kid, huh?"

"Yeah," I said, "some kid."

Then I walked back through the soft spring day, passing all the little kids and fast, spring-crazed dogs and gorgeous blooming flowers.

When I got back to where the Undesirable had been hanged, I noticed that a monarch butterfly was perched on the dead meat of his shoulder.

Somehow, it didn't look right.

3

On the way home, I had to stop for a funeral procession. There was a big black truck driving very slowly down the street. Behind it marched thirty or forty people all dressed in black. Some of them slapped little hollow tom-toms that made a dirge-like sound.

All the mourners wore black hoods that completely covered their faces.

After the original split between the Federation and the Zone, the Plague emerged. It seemed to be much worse in the Federation than the Zone. Nobody knew why.

The Plague started out like the flu, but six or seven days later you'd lost a third of your normal weight and had gone into shock. Most Plaguers didn't live longer than two weeks.

The same teenagers that liked to lynch Undesirables also liked to torch the houses where the Plague had struck.

That's why the mourners kept their faces covered, and why they were escorted by private guards with guns. So no teenagers could ambush them.

The Plague had taken more than ten percent of the population in the past fifteen years.

Federation scientists hadn't even been able to figure out how you got the Plague. At least not for sure. There were two or three prominent theories, but nobody knew if they were correct. Just last month, two prestigious Federation politicians had been struck down by the Plague. One of them even lost three sons to the disease.

I stood on the corner now, watching the black-hooded mourners march in back of the huge black van. The vans could store up to fifty bodies that would be burned on the edge of the city.

I remembered once when my little girl's fever soared one night and we spent three anxious days waiting to see if she simply had the stomach flu . . . or the Plague.

Fortunately, it had just been the flu.

Behind their masks, they wept and sobbed, the mourners making their slow but inexorable way to this burial by fire.

As terrible as the Federation was, I certainly didn't want to see its innocent children die from this awful disease.

4

That was Tuesday.

Thursday, I took the skimmer out to the field most Zone pilots fly out of. For fifteen percent of our gross, the people who run the field solicit work for us, handle all the financial transactions, and keep us apprised of which Zone areas are particularly hot—so we don't fly over them.

You get two kinds of Zone jobs.

The first is from customers who can't afford the big commercial flights. For these folks you haul everything from furniture to people. You're like a moving van that can fly. This is the bulk of the work.

But then there's a second kind, and that kind we don't talk much about: contraband. This can be anything from caches of dreamdust to spouses wanting to flee their husbands. People who want to disappear completely even offer to pay you large sums of money to take a shoot-down over the Zone. Then you can file papers saying that your passenger was killed but that you had no way of recovering the body. Then said passenger, very much alive, goes to the West Coast and starts his or her life all over again. The new lives are rarely as sweet as the person imagines, but then that's their problem, not mine.

I stayed up nearly an hour. Everything checked out well. Marvin had done his usual good, if overpriced, job.

I left the skimmer in its hangar slot. I went in search of an aircab and ran into Bronstein the scheduler.

"Got one for you. Needs to be in L.A. by next Tuesday at ten a.m. They specifically asked for you."

"You're kidding."

"That's what I thought. Some skinny little bald guy like you." He smiled. "Actually, my wife thinks you're cute. So maybe this one thinks you're cute, too."

"A woman, huh?"

"Yeah. Nice voice, too."

I needed the money. "I'll take it."

"The crate's over in the corner of your hangar. There's a lift there if nobody's around. I'll be able to add eight, nine other pieces by then."

We're paid on a per-piece basis. Obviously, you try and load up the cargo bay as much as possible.

"Thanks." Then, "Oh, and Bronstein?"

"Yeah?"

"Your wife's got good taste."

He laughed. "You asshole."

* * *

It took me a while, but I finally found an aircab to take me back to the urbanplex.

I went to my favorite bar for a relaxing drink, but it was a wrestling crowd that afternoon, and so Briney was forced to run contraband viddies of two four-armed Undesirables wrestling.

Federation law prohibits any exhibition of holos or the two-dimensional viddies that depict Undesirables in any form or fashion.

The ones that most people want are the sexual ones, of course. You get a female Undesirable with three breasts or her sex organ in an odd place, or you get a male Undesirable with two penises, and you've got a spellbound crowd.

"You never watch," Briney said.

"Nah," I said.

"Got a brother like you."

"Yeah?"

"Yeah. Hates muties so much, he won't even look at a pic of them. They just make his skin crawl."

I didn't tell him the reason *I* chose not to look. But I didn't figure he'd care anyway.

Briney runs a clean, safe neighborhood place where most of the Federation bureaucrats who live in the apartment complex come to drink. Mutant wrestling is about as wild as it ever gets.

He said, "So who is she?"

I glanced around. "She?"

"The woman."

"What woman?"

"What woman? You got so many women you

don't know what woman I'm talking about? Especially one that looks like her?"

"Believe it or not, Briney, I don't have a clue."

"You didn't miss her by more than fifteen minutes."

"And she was asking for me?"

He shrugged. "I wouldn't say asking *for* you exactly. More like asking *about* you, I guess."

"You tell her anything?"

He grinned. "Just that you're one hot stud that all the chicks really dig."

"Right."

"She was beautiful."

"Beautiful" isn't the kind of word a man like Briney uses very often. Women are cute or sexy or maybe even pretty. But women, in Briney's lexicon, are almost never beautiful.

"She asked if you were the Duvall who was a pilot."

"And you said—"

"That you were. And then she asked if you were the Duvall who had chartered a skimmer flight for Saturday afternoon. With a Ms. Saunders"

"And you said—"

"That I couldn't help her with that one."

"She ask anything else?"

"She asked if you'd mentioned anybody following you around lately?"

"And you said—"

"I said yeah. You told me about that redheaded

guy the other day, remember? The one they dragged into that aircar?"

"Yeah, I remember."

"She got kind of excited about that."

"She did?"

"Yeah. She asked if you'd seen the redheaded guy since then."

"So what'd you say to that?"

"I said I couldn't help her." He shook his head, as if marveling at a vision that danced before his eyes. "You should've seen her, Duvall."

"Beautiful, huh?"

"The kind you fall in love with."

"She have a name?"

"Not," said Briney, "that she was willing to share."

"So she just walked out?"

"She just walked out."

"Didn't say that she'd be back?"

"No, sir, she didn't. But I'd sure like to see her again."

Just then, the crowd around the viddie screen started whooping. From what I could gather, both muties had engaged all four of their arms simultaneously—eight arms for your ultimate wrestling pleasure.

I said good-bye to Briney, and left.

I was two blocks from the apartment house when he fell into step next to me. By magic, apparently. I hadn't sensed him behind me until too late.

"Hi," he said.

"Hi," I said.

"Mind if I walk with you? My name's Pete McClure, by the way."

"I have a feeling I don't have any choice."

"Good thing I'm not sensitive," he said. "A remark like that could hurt a guy's feelings."

"Yeah," I said, "I'll bet."

He was a cop. I just hadn't figured out what kind of cop he was, local or Federation, though I leaned toward the latter because of the chiseled face and crew cut.

He inhaled all of the pollutants and said, "This reminds me of the farm."

"You lived on a farm?"

He smiled. "A VR farm." The smile broadened. "That's how I defeated Napoleon, too."

"VR."

"Right."

I'd never gone for virtual reality much after I saw what happened to my brother. His VR fantasies become so fulfilling that he slowly started to reject reality. They tell you VR isn't addictive, but it is. My brother is currently under sedation in a Federation "retreat" where the patients are hosed down every morning in a communal shower.

Then: "She could be watching us right now, Mr. Duvall."

"Who could?"

"The woman we're looking for."

"Why would she be watching us?"

"Because you're the last person who saw Steve Ford before he disappeared.

We walked some more. A small dog came up and danced around in circles and yipped up at me. I petted him a few times.

"Steve Ford is the man who followed you the other day."

"I see."

"We were following him while he was following you."

"This just seems to get more complicated, doesn't it?"

He said, "They're enemies of the state, Mr. Duvall. Both the man and the woman."

Enemies of the state. There was a nice pompous phrase. Now I knew for sure what kind of cop he was. Federation.

"I don't know why they'd want me."

"Neither do we, Mr. Duvall. And that's why we're keeping you under surveillance." He paused. "We think that they can ultimately lead us to Keeler."

"I thought Keeler was dead."

"That's what the Front wants us to believe. But we have reason to believe that he's alive and living on the West Coast somewhere. He's most likely had a complete transform."

Transforms are safer than they used to be. Early on, a number of people, including a few famous ones, died on the operating table. Several of the injections used are lethal if the prescribed dosage is exceeded by even .000007 mg. The most remarkable transform I'd seen was changing a black woman into a white man.

By now, Keeler, if he really was alive, could look like 100,000 different people.

We walked a short block in silence.

We reached the point where the Undesirable had been hanging the other day. All evidence of him was gone. The local cops leave the bodies up there just long enough to send a message. Then the corpses are cut down and taken away and burned in a huge oven on the northernmost edge of the urbanplex. Sometimes, on hot days especially, you can smell the flesh if you get anywhere near it.

"I'm afraid we haven't been able to find out much about your politics, Mr. Duvall."

"That's because I don't *have* any politics."

"A cynic. That's always sad to see, Mr. Duvall."

"Not a cynic. Just somebody who doesn't like to waste his time voting when there's only one party running."

"We must've seen different ballots, then, Mr. Duvall. On my ballot, there were four parties running."

"Uh-huh. And every one of them was a front for the Federation."

I saw his blue eyes narrow slightly.

He was a good and true foot soldier. Even hint that you did not share his faith in his employers, and all his internal security alarms went off.

"Maybe it's time for a Weekend, Mr. Duvall."

The Federation, ever eager to prove how benign it is, has set up special Weekends for all citizens who express serious doubts about the prevailing political system. You get good food, a lovely view of the Rockies, and enough deep-psych "adjustment" to keep you blissed out the rest of your life.

We were in front of my apartment house now, one-hundred-and-twenty-nine stories of safe, secure living.

Armed guards and crazed black dogs patrolled the perimeters of the place. On every tenth floor, a guard with a laser rifle frowned down upon the grounds. The corporation boasted that no burglar had ever attempted to penetrate the defenses of this place. I believed them.

I held up my palm. The guard aimed a scanner at it. A tiny beep sounded in the scanner. My ID had checked out.

I said to the cop: "I meant it when I said I wasn't political. I don't like the Federation and I don't like the Front, all right?"

"And if either of these people should try to contact you—"

"I'll get hold of you right away."

"I can take your word for that?"

"Absolutely."

"They're dangerous, reckless people, Mr. Duvall."

"And I'll take *your* word for that."

He put out a hand. It was cold and slab-hard.

Maybe he was one of the new androids that the newsies were so excited about.

"You may not like the Federation government much," the cop said as his final word. "But try to imagine what kind of world it would be without it."

Then he turned around in a curt, military way, and made his way down the long walkway to the street.

A dark blue skimmer with smoked windows swooped down, picked him up, and took him away.

5

At night, Briney's place has been known to house women on the lookout for men. I have been told this for nearly three years now. I have never experienced this for myself.

I had three drinks too quickly and then had to have a peminin pill to insure the return of sobriety. Briney was not enamored of drunks.

I spent most of my time thinking about the Federation cop I'd met this afternoon. Who was the red-haired man? And who was the woman looking for me? Briney's was dark, and there wasn't all that many people, and so it was a good place to brood.

Around nine, two guys at the opposite end of the bar strapped vid visors on their heads. A beeper had gone off indicating an important story on the news holos.

Seeing this, Briney punched up the wall holo.

The shot was from a police skimmer.

Three people, two men and a woman, were running along the pier, a half-dozen police dogs coming after them relentlessly.

The announcer: "Now this breaking story. Three Undesirables who earlier escaped a police dragnet have now been spotted on Langdon Pier, an industrial part of Langdon Bay. Police dogs are closing in."

You could see what the three criminals had in mind. Reach the end of the pier and jump into the water. They couldn't jump in now because there were warehouses on their right and ten-foot-high fencing on their left. They needed to reach the end of the pier.

They had maybe twenty feet to go when the dogs caught them.

That's when I went over and played the loudest VR game I could find. There was a good one about an Old West shootout. I was the outsider and I happened upon a party of Native Americans intent on slaying me and my friends. This was the action version. In the sexual version (and you got your choice, hetero, homo, or both, me taking hetero), the Native Americans happened to be fetching young women who rode naked upon their war ponies. They captured me and took me back to their tepees where they solaced my body in silken ways that were pleasurable in the extreme.

When I got done, the crowd was standing around the wall holo.

They always ran the best parts of the viddie over and over.

In this case, that meant the part where the dogs

began to rend and rip the bodies of the Undesirables they'd captured.

"Man, you see that fuckin' dog with the arm between his teeth? How'd you like to meet that sonofabitch in an alley some night?"

"That one dog just ripped her nose off. You see that? Just ripped her nose right off."

And so on.

I thought about leaving, but then the door opened up and the woman came in and I knew it was her.

We watched each other for what seemed a long time but was probably just a few seconds.

"Guess who?" Briney said.

"Yeah."

She kept right on watching me.

"You want a couple of drinks?"

"Yeah."

I kept right on watching her.

"You want me to bring 'em back to that little table in front of the VR games?"

"Yeah."

We kept right on watching each other.

"If I didn't know better, Duvall, I'd say you were in love."

I went back to the table and she followed me about ten paces behind.

We sat down but didn't say anything until Briney brought the drinks and left.

I kept thinking of how Briney had called her beautiful. I also kept thinking about how beautiful didn't do her justice, not that tumbling

midnight hair, and those cheekbones and mouth
that hinted of an arrogance the huge brown sad
eyes belied. She wore a white Federation jumper
that gave her long body an unexpected and aston-
ishing elegance, Federation jumpers not exactly
being on the cutting edge of high fashion.

She sipped her drink and said, "You don't
know what any of this is about yet, do you?"

"No, I guess I don't."

"It's about a girl." She paused. Looked at me
with her solemn eyes. "The girl is my daughter."

"I see."

"I know about your daughter, Mr. Duvall. And
about your wife." She paused. "What they were, I
mean. And how they died."

"Is this some kind of trap?"

"No. We're on the same side."

"I don't have a side."

She hesitated, looked down at her drink, and
then back up at me.

"I'm sure you loved them."

"They were my life."

"That's why you should help us, Mr. Duvall.
We're trying to win freedom for everybody, Normals and Undesirables alike. The only way the
Federation keeps power is by exploiting the fear
that Normals have for Undesirables. They've persecuted us long enough."

"Us?" I said. "You're an Undesirable?"

"Not me, personally, no. But my father—"

"I see."

"He went undetected, but it wasn't an easy life.

My mother and father were frightened all their lives. Every time somebody came to the door, we thought—"

She didn't have to finish.

I knew exactly what she was talking about.

You live with a hunted feeling. I had, anyway, always waiting for my wife or daughter to be found out, for the Federation forces to swoop down.

My daughter had been knocked out playing a game of Pom-Pon Pullaway one day. Tripped, and stumbled into a tree, and hit her head.

Her friend accidentally pulled her blouse up while trying to get Dori back on her feet. Beneath the blouse, to the right of Dori's spine, lay the dead green eye.

Her friend ran home, leaving Dori there on the ground, and told her mother.

Her teenage brother and his friends happened to be there. They knew fun when they saw it.

I'd just pulled my landcar into the drive after work. It was dusk. They hid in the garage.

They got me at gunpoint and forced me inside.

The next few hours aren't clear. They checked me out. Because they couldn't find any sign of mutation on me, they couldn't legally kill me. All they could do was keep knocking me out, so I couldn't stop them from their legal pleasures.

They raped my wife and daughter several times. Dori was nine years old.

When they'd tired of the games, they took

Sharon and Dori outside and hanged them from the big maple tree on our front lawn.

When the Federation police did get there, they took me to a Reawakening Center, where I spent the next six weeks of my life. The Reawakening Center endeavored to make me sorry that I had betrayed my own kind by shielding mutants, and by helping the Front to prosper.

The Front was the radical fringe of the Undesirable movement. Every few months, they'd blow up a Federation building, usually a hospital or a school. They'd killed more than 20,000 innocent Normals in the past five years.

I didn't agree with their methods any more than I did the methods of the Normals.

She said, "My name's Anne, by the way."

"This week."

"Pardon?"

"This week your name's Anne. What was it last week?"

She smiled. "Penelope." Then: "I can't believe you're not sympathetic to the Front."

"All political groups are the same. They all claim to help everyday, average folks. But what they really want is power. They're all corrupt, and they're all bloodthirsty."

"The Front only does what it has to."

"Yeah, like blow up hospitals with little kids in it?"

She frowned. "I don't see how you can defend the Federation after what happened to your wife and daughter."

"I'm not defending the Federation. I hate them. But I hate what the Front does, too. People have to give up killing each other before they can sit down and talk."

"You're very smug, Mr. Duvall."

"So are you."

"I'm afraid you're going to help me, even if you don't want to."

"Oh?"

"In my right hand I have a stunner, Mr. Duvall."

"I see."

"I want you to walk out the door with me right now."

"And if I don't"

"Then I'll kill you."

"All in the name of the Front?"

"All in the name of the people, Mr. Duvall, the people who are being tortured and persecuted every day of their lives."

She had all her lines down smooth and slick and unwavering. True believers usually do. After the murders of my wife and daughter, I was contacted by a few Front people. They gave me the impression that there was nothing quite so thrilling as giving little revolutionary speeches. They probably enjoyed hearing themselves talk even more than they enjoyed having sex.

I was reasonably sure she *would* shoot me.

I stood up.

"Front door or back?"

She smiled. "Who knows, Mr. Duvall, maybe

you'll want to help us someday of your own free will."

"I doubt it."

Briney was there.

"I was just going to ask if you wanted another round," he said, his eyes taking in her graceful body as she stood up.

"We're leaving," I said.

He looked at me and then at her and then back at me.

He winked. He must have been hanging around with Marvin.

He didn't seem to notice the small bulge in the right-hand pocket of her Federation jumpsuit.

"You two kids have a good time," Briney said.

I thought of pushing him into her and going out the back door. But the odds were long against me, and I just might get Briney killed in the process. Or myself.

A lot of the male drinkers followed her progress to the door with devout and unsettled attention.

She really was a heartbreaker, a true ethereal beauty.

Physically, anyway.

Mentally, she was hard, ugly, and absolutely convinced of her own righteousness. Hitler had had such followers, and Senator McCarthy, and Charles Manson, and a lot of religious leaders who advocated killing people only because God had told them it was necessary. She'd been hurt as a child—it couldn't have been any fun fearing that your parents would be murdered at any moment—but she hadn't learned any compassion or empathy from it. She'd learned only hatred and vengeance. She was a sad and dangerous woman. You can excuse any atrocity if you just feel sorry enough for yourself.

There was a misty rain waiting for us, the night streets shiny with it. In the distance, the sounds of sirens—some emergency, some illness or injury that will be our own someday.

"Around back."

"Maybe you don't have a stunner in that pocket."

She whipped it out and put it in my face.

"Satisfied?"

She shoved the stunner back in her pocket and moved slightly ahead of me.

The first shot took off a piece of the roof of the landcar to her left.

The scorching smell of a laser blast—a stunner set up high, maybe ten or eleven, easily enough to kill both of us.

I pushed her to the ground and glanced around the lot.

I didn't see much of him, just the nose and eyes and the top of the head, but enough to know who he was: the red-haired man who'd followed me to Marvin's the other day. Steve Ford.

Who the hell was he? Why the hell did he want to kill us?

She got off a few shots of her own.

She was good, but not great, ripping up the

roofs of a couple of cars as he ducked and bobbed behind them, circling wide to get a better shot at us.

She came close enough on her fourth shot to make him cry out with a curse.

Then it was his turn.

He finished circling, and then did a couple of numbers he must have picked up from some old Errol Flynn holos.

He jumped up on the roof of one landcar and then started walking across the roofs of several others, all the time firing his stunner and scorching up all kinds of glass and rubber and alloy.

All this kept us pinned down, of course.

His flamboyance and recklessness was scary to watch.

"I want her back, Sara."

He said that when he was only two car roofs away from us.

I didn't know what he was talking about, only that he was addressing the woman next to me.

They knew each other? What the hell was this all about?

We kept crouched down, glancing left and right for an escape route.

But up high that way, he could see us without much trouble.

He could fire down on us before she could fire up at him.

Night and rain and the almost obscene laughter of the crowd inside Briney's and the sweet smell of her sweat, the sweat of fear, and the hammering of my heart ... this was my only reality for perhaps ten seconds.

He was silent.

Unmoving.

I wondered what he was up to.

And then I knew.

Sara and I were facing westward, waiting for him to appear on the roof of the landcar we were hiding behind.

But he was clever.

He'd snuck down off the landcar and then tip-toed around in back of us.

He said, standing no more than two feet from us, "Put the stunner away, Sara."

"You bastard," she said, even before she'd turned completely around.

"All I want to know is where she is," he said.

She turned and faced him, and then did to me what I'd decided not to do to Briney inside.

She pushed me into the red-haired man. He would have to shoot me to get at her.

She had just enough room, and just enough time, for a good clean shot at his face, and she took it.

This close, her stunner set on the high side, his features collapsed into a kind of bloody pudding.

He fell backward, stunner flying off to the side, a scream strangling inside his throat.

The sour smell of burned flesh gagged me.

"You really needed to kill him?" I said.

"You don't think he would've killed us?" she said, going over to him.

"He had a chance, and he didn't take it. He just wanted to know where 'she' was. Whoever 'she' is."

But Sara wasn't listening.

She was bent over the body going through his Federation jumpsuit with quick skill and ease.

She didn't find anything.

"Bastard," she said.

The back door opened then and I saw three male customers walking out into the misty night.

They saw us right away, saw the body sprawled out dead, and then ran right over.

"Hey, what the hell's going on here?" the biggest one said.

Sara was going to run. It was in her eyes and face.

She turned and started away, but I grabbed her and whispered, "Who the hell was he, anyway?"

And she said, "My husband. Now let go of me."

Then she started walking away, trying to seem calm, but moving faster and faster as she reached the shadows of the alley.

"This a robbery or what?" the big customer said.

"Yeah, that's what it was," I said, "a robbery."

One of his buddies went in to phone the police.

6

I didn't see McClure until I actually reached the police station. The computer had apparently flagged my name and when he saw it involved in Steve Ford's death, he left the warmth of home and hearth and came down to the cold, hard station to see me.

There'd been a flash riot of some kind. A lot of teenagers nursing bloody wounds and sneers were in the front of the station being booked by a robot that was also spraying them down for various diseases. Most of the riots are about drugs flown in from the Zone. Zone drugs are the best and most expensive, and therefore lead to the most violence. That was another thing I didn't like about the Front. Most of their violence was sponsored by drug money they got from addicting the children of Normals.

"You know what I was doing?" McClure said when we were seated all nice and friendly in his tiny office with the baby pictures all over the wall. His baby girls were heartbreakers.

"You got me."

"Playing patty-cake with my one-year-old. She couldn't sleep. Middle of the night, she still wants to play patty-cake."

"Cute."

"You had a daughter once."

"Right."

"I know what happened."

"Good for you."

"I'm not belittling you, Mr. Duvall. If one of my daughters had been born— Well, I probably would do the same thing you did."

It was cop bullshit. The better ones used psychology instead of fits or drugs.

"Sara Ford has a daughter, too."

"She does, huh?" I said.

"She didn't tell you about it when you were in Briney's with her?"

"I guess she mentioned it."

"Her daughter is a very special girl."

"She mentioned that, too."

"A lot of people want to get their hands on her."

"Including the Federation?"

He nodded. "I won't bullshit you."

"Thanks."

"We want her desperately. The girl."

"How old is she?"

"Fourteen."

"What's so special about her?"

"Sara Ford didn't tell you?"

"No."

He leaned back in his chair. With his short hair

and his open face, he looked like the perfect young husband and father. Life would be simple for him. He didn't know how lucky he was. Or maybe in my self-pity I was kidding myself. Maybe life isn't simple for anybody, not even the luckiest of us.

"I wish I could tell you about the girl, but I can't."

This surprised me and my face must have reflected my surprise.

"Strange, huh, that I can't even tell you why we want her? That's how classified the whole matter is."

He turned and said a code word and a portion of the west wall became a holo screen.

A very pretty young girl was there. She resembled Sara Ford except for the eyes.

"She's blind?"

"Yes."

"From birth?"

"We think so."

He watched me a long moment.

"You don't like them, do you, Mr. Duvall? The Front, I mean?"

"No, I don't. But I don't like the Federation any better. You both exploit people to stay in power."

"At least we don't blow up hospitals with children in them."

"Yes, but you let lynching Undesirables go on night and day."

"I guess that's a fair point."

He opened a desk drawer and took out a cylinder no larger than a fountain pen. It was silver.

"Know what this is?"

"Truth probe?"

"Exactly."

"You sure you know how to use it?"

He smiled. "I use it all the time, Mr. Duvall. Those stories you hear are mostly exaggerations. Fortunately."

You always hear how ill-trained cops burn out people's brains using too much power in the probes.

"All you need to do is sit still and close your eyes, Mr. Duvall. I've only got eight questions to ask you. Shouldn't take long at all."

I sat still and closed my eyes.

I was nervous.

I couldn't help it.

Visions of my brains being fried kept filling the dark screen before my eyes.

"Ready?"

"Ready," I said.

Afterward, I checked the wall chrono. I'd been out six minutes. A slight trickle of blood ran from my nose.

McClure pushed a box of wipers at me.

"The blood's nothing to worry about. About a third of the people who get probed get bloody noses."

I got the blood stopped as much as I could, then pushed his wiper box back to him.

"She kill him in cold blood?"

"He shot at us first."

"She have to kill him?"

"You didn't ask me these questions when you probed me?"

He shook his head. "All I wanted the probe for was to recreate the conversation you'd had with her. You let her down. She wanted to turn you into a Front foot soldier."

"I meant what I told her. I don't have any sides in this particular war."

"She'll contact you again."

"I suppose."

"Somehow you're going to help with her daughter. She was probably going to tell you that later tonight. But then Ford showed up."

"All I want to do is get back to work."

"She have to kill him?"

"I suppose not."

"She's a tough cookie, Mr. Duvall. That god-damned face of hers can break your heart. But inside she's all vampire, believe me. She's probably killed twenty Federation agents in the last five years."

I said, "I won't spy for you."

"You're clever, Mr. Duvall. That was going to be the next thing I asked you."

"The answer's no."

"You could save a lot of lives."

"So could you if you'd make it illegal to lynch Undesirables."

"I don't make the law, Mr. Duvall."

I sighed. "I won't spy."

"What happens if she contacts you?"

"I tell her I don't want to get involved. On either side."

"And then?"

"Then I go back to Zone flying, and back to my life."

"It's not much of a life, if you'll pardon my saying so."

"I had a life once. The Federation helped take it away from me."

"I'm sorry about that. I really am."

"Yeah."

"We'll be following you."

"I know that."

"We may use you as bait to trap her."

"If I don't know about it in advance, then I guess I'll just have to let you use me as bait."

"She'd kill you if she found out. You don't know what she's like, Mr. Duvall. You're taken with her looks and that's very, very dangerous, believe me."

"I'll remember that."

"I appreciate your coming down."

"I didn't have any choice."

He stood up and put out his hand.

"I'd like to end on a friendly note if possible, Mr. Duvall."

I shook his hand without quite knowing why.

When I was at the door, he said, "I shouldn't have said that you don't have much of a life,

Mr. Duvall. That was pretty arrogant of me to make a judgment like that."

"Yes," I said, "it was."

I left.

7

A few miles from the hangar there's a combination general store and bar that caters to Zoners, as Zone pilots call themselves. Reb, the owner, is a former Zoner himself. He likes to enumerate all the body parts he lost during his flying days: one eye, part of an ear, two fingers, one testicle, a big toe, and a large chunk of his considerable ass. He has a beard and a belly, and if he's ever washed the mercenary uniform he wears all the time, he hasn't let anybody else know about it.

Not having flown while I was recuperating, I was badly in need of supplies, which Reb was only too happy to supply to me.

"You hear about the cannibals?" he said as we walked down the aisles of merchandise and I threw stuff into my cart.

"This sounds like one of your gags," I said. Reb loved jokes. Bad ones.

"No shit, man. Honest-to-God cannibals. You remember Wiggins?"

"Black guy?"

"Yeah. Him and Dorsey, they got downed

couple months ago, not too long after you did. And guess what? They seen this band of kids comin' after 'em—goddamned little kids, man— and the kids catch Dorsey and they eat him. Just tore him right apart with their hands and teeth."

"How'd Wiggins escape?"

"Made it to this cave and found this underground stream. Said he felt guilty about leavin' Dorsey behind after the kids wounded him, but he didn't have no choice. You know how it goes."

"They use ketchup?"

Reb made a face.

"God, you're really a wiseass, Duvall, you know it?"

"Not really. Just if I don't joke about it, I'd go crazy."

He grinned with his bad teeth.

"Zoners're crazy, anyway. Didn't you know that?"

After I picked up medical supplies, blankets, a new rifle, and a new stunner, and after Reb agreed to have them delivered to my hangar, we went into the bar where he treated me to a drink. The walls are filled with holos of various mutants Zoners saw and photographed after their skimmers were shot down.

This was a day to remember.

Reb isn't known for his charity.

I was halfway through my first Scotch when some perfume that smelled familiar made me angle my head to the right and there she was.

"Hey, Duvall," Betsy said.

"Hey."

"You don't look any uglier than you did before the crash."

"Thanks for the compliment."

There's a standing joke among Zoners—if you think male Zoners are ugly, wait until you meet the female Zoners.

It is not a calling that attracts the fey, the epicene, or those inclined to an appreciation for ballet. Of any sex.

The men are men, and so are the women, as another of the Zoner jokes goes.

Betsy was an exception.

She was five feet four and cute and delicate as the girl you had your first third grade crush on.

"How's Phil?" I said.

She grinned. "Who?"

"You finally dump him?"

She frowned. Cutely. "He dumped me the day before I was going to dump him. So, technically, I guess he broke my heart."

"Technically, huh?"

"He was just what you said he was."

"What did I say he was?"

"An ass-bandit who'd break my heart."

"I was just jealous."

"I know. But you were still right about him."

Betsy had dated me, God knows why, for a month or so and I'd started getting funny possessive ideas that made her extremely nervous.

Then one night this West Coast Zoner named

Phil breezes in, all long curly black hair and slick leather Zone outfit, and he just took her away right on the spot.

Looking at her now, looking carefully at her eyes I mean, I could see that he'd broken her heart in more ways than technically.

Then I glanced down at the edge of her left-hand sleeve.

"What the hell's that?"

"Aw, shit," she said, and tugged her sleeve down. "How about just buying me a drink and keeping your big Irish mouth shut?"

I leaned in so I could whisper.

"You cut your wrist over that candy-ass bastard?"

The tears in her eyes answered my question.

I ordered us two Scotches.

She grabbed them both and gunned them.

"Ladies first," she said.

She was snuffling back the tears.

"I need a lift to L.A.," she said after I'd ordered us more drinks. "I'm told you're leaving tomorrow."

"Yeah. But what's wrong with your skimmer?"

"Had to sell it."

"How come?"

She shrugged.

"I was, uh, in this dreamdust ward."

Dreamdust is the primary drug the Front supplies Normals.

"That's bad stuff."

"I don't need any lectures, Pop."

"All because of that dumb-ass pilot," I said.

"Well," she said. "You got all hot and bothered over me. And that was pretty dumb, if you don't mind my saying so."

"I didn't end up in any dreamdust ward."

She reached over and took my big hand with her little one. Her little one was shaking. Bad.

"So can I hitch?"

"Sure."

"No lectures."

Looking at her now, I was afraid I was going to get tears in *my* eyes. The dumb, goddamned little kid.

The place was filling up. I still had to go plot my course. Plan the trip itself.

"I shouldn't have said that, Duvall. About it being dumb that you had a crush on me that time."

"That's all right."

"It was kind of cute, actually."

"Yeah."

"You're just not my type is all."

I slugged back my drink.

"I leave at four a.m. sharp, hangar 17-B."

"You pissed about something, Duvall?"

"Nah," I said. "I guess not."

It seemed a good time to get, so I got.

Forty-three years ago a little biotech company in Winnetka, Illinois, got broken into by two burglars who were about to change all history. Their names were Rasmussen and Edmonds. You can look them up on the history software. They're in there, all right.

What the two hapless burglars did—after robbing the place of its modest supply of cash—was trash the place.

No particular reason.

They were young and drugged and stupid with, I imagine, an emphasis on the latter.

And in trashing the place, they smashed a glass cage that held an experimental biogenetically engineered virus.

This was the mother of all germ warfare.

The little lab hoped to sell it to the United States Government, and retire on the proceeds.

What the owners of the lab hadn't anticipated was two nickel-dime clowns like Rasmussen and Edmonds breaking into their place and loosing their virus on our country. They hadn't been satisfied with breaking the glass cage. They had to smash the canister, too.

J-K4 was the official name of the virus. Later on people called it Jake4.

In the next twenty-four hours, more than 200,000 children, women, and men died horrible deaths. The Ebola virus had nothing on Jake4. Ebola liquified all your internal organs. This turned you, inside *and* out, into a kind of blood pudding.

A quarantine area was set up, and it was quite an area. All the states that hugged the Pacific were fine, as were all the states that hugged the Atlantic.

Everything else, however, was in quarantine, and remains that way today.

Eventually, after roughly ten years, the virus was contained.

But by then the quarantine area had come to be known as the Zone, and it was a nation unto itself, the human species there having mutated into dozens of grotesque, terrifying, sad, comic, bedazzling forms.

Anybody who lived in the Zone was known as an Undesirable.

Those Undesirables who felt they could pass as Normals frequently crossed into the Federation states and tried to live Normal lives.

But most of them were found out sooner or later, and then hanged. Or burned. Or mutilated. Teenage lynch mobs were resourceful and inventive slayers of anybody different from themselves.

From all this misery and strife came the Front, the Undesirable terrorist group that meant to bring down the Federation, and integrate the Zone with the Federation states.

I was all for this.

What I was against was the methods the Front used.

They were just as ruthless with Normals as Normals were with Undesirables.

For me, a choice between one terrorist group and another was no choice at all.

* * *

I was just checking out the cargo manifold when I heard a familiar voice.

"She hasn't made contact."

McClure made it a statement rather than a question.

"No, she hasn't," I said.

The hangar smelled of grease and sunlight.

Two robots off-loaded a few tons of boxes into the cargo hold.

The robots were programmed to sing as they worked.

They were not gifted singers, these robots.

"You leave tomorrow?" he said.

"Uh-huh."

"Four a.m.?"

"Uh-huh."

He nodded to the cargo hold.

"We scanned everything this morning. Hope you don't mind."

"Didn't find anything?"

"Nothing suspicious."

He paused.

"We're just wondering how she's going to use you."

"Now you're getting *me* curious," I said.

He walked around the skimmer.

"Nice craft."

"Yeah, I like it."

"You a little nervous about going over the Zone again?"

"A little, I suppose."

He said, "Cannibals."

"Yeah. I heard."

"Man, can you imagine that? Eating human flesh?" He shuddered.

Then he walked over by the cargo bay and said, "You know the one we were real interested in?"

"The first piece of cargo I got for this flight, probably. The woman who asked for me to be the pilot."

"Right."

"So what did the scan show?"

"Fabric."

"Sounds exciting."

"We've been out here checking every three, four hours, seeing if anything new's come in."

"And nothing, huh?"

"No sign of her," McClure said. "Or the kid."

I said, "I wonder what the hell she's up to."

McClure grinned. "If you find out, let me know, huh? The wife's p.g. again, and I'm gonna be needing a raise here real soon."

"I'll do what I can, McClure."

Then I went back to my cargo manifold, and McClure went back to making people's lives miserable.

8

McClure's people followed me around the rest of the day. A couple of times I couldn't help myself, and I'd wave to them when I came out of a particular store. One of them was a real smartass. He waved back.

My last stop for the day was at LASER CITY, where I got my stunner recharged. This took half an hour; while I waited, I started looking over the new models.

I took a Force-5 stunner over to the range to try it out. I was just sighting it in relation to the target when a familiar voice said, "I wanted to put in a good word for us."

I lowered the gun and looked over at Briney.

"You should be working, Briney."

"Needed to talk to you."

"How'd you know I was out here?"

"Been following around McClure's guy. Asshole waved back at you. I couldn't believe it."

You can know somebody a long time without "knowing" him in any way. Or even being curious about him, I suppose.

I'd been going to Briney's place for several years. In all that time, I hadn't learned much about his life or his interests. Ours was a simple relationship. He provided the booze, and I drank it.

"You followed me?"

"Uh-huh."

"Why?"

"Because I want to put in a good word for her."

"Who's 'her'?"

He looked around, suddenly suspicious. LASER CITY was one big warehouse filled with everything from teeny tiny scanners that could fit into your boots to laser shotguns that could disintegrate a small house.

The place was packed today. The Federation had really been riding the holos heavy about the real and imagined threat from the Front. Normals were told they needed weapons to defend themselves and their cause.

"You know who I'm talking about," he said. Then leaned in: "Sara."

"Sara Ford?"

"God, Duvall, not so loud."

I whispered: "How do you know Sara?"

His doughy face frowned. "How do you think?"

I looked at him a long time.

Then I realized what he was.

Very softly, I said: "You're an Undesirable?"

Very softly, he replied: "Eight toes."

"Aw, shit."

He looked scared a moment. "You going to turn me in?"

"Of course not. But—"

I shook my head, tried to gather myself.

"Let's take a walk around the store."

He nodded.

As we walked, we could speak in fairly normal voices. There were so many guns being demonstrated, and so many people talking, nobody was likely to overhear us.

A lot of the sales personnel, human and robot alike, were decked out as cowboys.

There were a lot of hero-white outfits, complete with fringe, spangles, and big white hats. And there were a lot of villain-black outfits, complete with black eyepatches and big black hats.

"You put Sara Ford on to me, didn't you?" I said.

"Yeah," he said. "You were always a little vague about your past. So one night, I probed you when you didn't know it, and found out about your wife and daughter. You seemed like a good man to have on our side. You being a Zoner, and all."

"So you told Sara about me?"

"Uh-huh."

"And she thinks I'm going to fly her across the Zone?"

"You're the most likely candidate. You're one of us."

"No, I'm not."

"That's what you say. But deep down—"

"Deep down, I think the Federation *and* the Front are screwed up. I don't want anything to do with you."

"The Front isn't what you think. Most of us are pretty decent people."

"Yeah, except when you're blowing up hospitals."

"Only three hospitals."

"Gee, I'm proud of you, Briney," I said. "Only three hospitals when it could have been so many more."

"This is the gun that killed Jesse James," a robot said as we passed him. "Authentic down to the last detail."

Yeah, I thought. Bob Ford really surprised Jesse that warm Missouri afternoon when he pulled a laser gun on him.

When we got to the end of the aisle, I said to Briney, "I hope you realize you lost a customer."

He stared at me earnestly, and in that moment I saw something in Briney I'd never even suspected. Briney was a very sad guy. I looked at the whipped-dog brown eyes and the wan mouth and the slumped shoulders, and I realized that I've never really looked at Briney before. He was bartender, I was customer.

"The way we're treated, Duvall, it ain't right. We're people, too. We didn't ask to be born this way."

I couldn't take looking at his tears.

I grabbed a handgun and pretended to give it an incredibly close inspection.

"Don't put this on me, Briney," I insisted. "I don't want to get involved."

"Your own goddamned wife and your own goddamned daughter," he said. "And you don't want to get involved."

I put the gun down and looked at him again.

"She's just as crazy as the Federation."

"She can be a little excessive at times."

"A little excessive? She killed her own husband in cold blood."

"You don't know the whole story."

"I don't *need* to know the whole story, Briney. I saw her kill him."

Just then a couple of robots came square-dancing their way down the aisle.

They didn't leave much room for us.

The female robot, all got up in a calico dress and a little white hat, was actually cute in a strange way.

"I can't help you, Briney," I said, after the robots had do-si-doed past us.

"Your own wife and daughter," he said.

"You said that already, Briney."

He looked even sadder than he had before. He'd come here to recruit me, to help transport Sara and her daughter across the Zone.

He'd failed, and was unhappy.

"I thought you were a friend of mine," he said.

"No, you didn't. You thought I was somebody you could use."

And with that, I left him there, the robots do-si-doing their way down another aisle, the pitchman telling his small crowd about this being the "authentic" stunner that was used to kill Jesse James, and the main exit looking awfully good to me just then.

Didn't sleep well. Anxiety about the flight, I suppose. Easy enough to say that you're eager to get back in the skimmer and fly over the Zone again.

But once you get shot down, you realize how close you are to death any time you're over the Zone.

You have the beamer, of course, and that's helpful in terms of summoning emergency help.

But the crash could kill you.

And then there's the Zone itself.

Just because my wife and daughter had small mutations, and just because I was in sympathy with mutants and wanted to see them integrated into Federation society, didn't mean I was up to dealing with any of the myriad freaks who roamed the Zone, some harmful, some not.

It was still dark when I got up, shaved, showered, and got an aircab to get me to my hangar.

I strolled in right at 4:10 a.m. and saw a cute little bottom sticking out of the cargo door.

"You're late," Betsy said, turning around and jumping down from the hold.

She brushed her hands together and said, "There was some extra cargo, so I loaded it up."

"If I had an award, I'd give it to you."

She looked me up and down.

"You nervous?"

"Nah."

"Right," she said.

"Well, a little, I suppose."

"Nothing to be ashamed of, Duvall. Getting shot down is scary."

"You ever get shot down?"

"Huh-uh. But this gal I roomed with was. She had nightmares about it for a couple of years." Then: "By the way, there was a Federation agent here till a couple minutes ago. He checked out all the new cargo"

One of McClure's people, I thought. Cargo would have been off-loaded all during the night, as it arrived.

"My Federation friends," I said. I hadn't told her about Sara Ford yet.

She looked at the skimmer.

"Marvin check this out?"

"Checked it out and brought it up to speed," I said.

"You want to push it out on the runway?"

"Gotta get all the papers first."

Donald was in the big office where they check out all the skimmer pilots.

Another two hours, he'd be going home.

He kept looking up at the chrono every half minute or so.

"Need all the stuff for landing in L.A.," I told him.

"I don't know why we bother. They just throw all this shit away, anyway."

"Are you serious?"

"Friend of mine used to work on the check-in desk. Said they'd take all this stuff and pitch it out the back door."

"I thought they had to keep it on file, you know, in case they had to cross-reference it sometime."

He shook his head. Donald looks like an old-time fire-and-brimstone minister who is always mightily displeased with the behavior of his fellow human beings. He was, in fact, a minister for many years, and then gave it up for a romantic job in air cargo.

"Betsy said she's going with you," Donald said.

"Yeah."

"I know a lot of guys who'd like to be alone with her up there," he said. I don't think I'd ever heard him make a suggestive remark before. I wanted to slap him on the back and congratulate him. Then: "Maybe you'll have more luck this time."

"This time?"

"Yeah. You know, maybe she won't dump you this time."

"Who said she dumped me?"

"Are you kidding? Everybody said she dumped you."

"Everybody?"

"Yeah, guys sit around and talk about Betsy, they always talk about what a heartbreaker she is. I mean, it's not just you she dumped."

"She didn't dump me."

"If you say so."

"We just decided not to go out anymore."

"Uh-huh."

He was irritating me, but there wasn't much I could do about it.

People believe what they want to about you, and they don't let facts get in the way.

She really hadn't dumped me.

Not exactly, anyway.

He did this thing with the papers and the computers and the big official stamp that makes everything good and legal, and then he handed them all over to me with just a touch of bureaucratic ceremony.

"She's got a great ass," he said.

"I'll mention it to her."

"I already did."

Could this be the prim, proper Donald I'd known all these years?

Maybe I'd made as many wrong assumptions about him as he'd made about me.

"She's got a nice little pair of charlies, too," he said as I was walking over to the door.

I turned around and looked at him.

"Donald, aren't you ashamed of yourself for talking that way?"

"Hell, no," he said, "that's why I gave up being a minister. So I could talk this way and not feel guilty."

His grin, or maybe it was a leer, made him look twenty years younger.

9

We rolled the skimmer out on the runway.

Everything smelled impossibly fresh. Dew was silver on the grass in the fading moonlight. Our shadows played like children on the runway as we did the standard last-minute mechanical check.

In the cockpit, I checked out all the instruments, tested the communication system with the tower, and then tried the emergency chute.

All the time, I kept thinking about Sara Ford, and how she hadn't been able to use me, after all.

McClure had stayed too close.

Betsy climbed into the copilot's seat.

"This isn't a bad little buggy at all," she said.

"Thanks for your approval."

"God, you're sensitive."

"Well, if you think I'm bad now, wait till I wake up."

She chucked me on the arm.

"All I meant was that it isn't real, you know, fast."

"It isn't?"

"Not compared to the rigs I fly, it isn't."

Night was retreating; rose started staining the sky now.

"You ready?" I asked.

"Uh-huh."

I did all the things you're supposed to do to this particular type of craft, and damned if they didn't work, just like the instructional holo had said they would.

We still hadn't gone anywhere but we were a lot closer now.

Then Betsy said: "Wait!"

"What?"

"They're bringing out some more cargo."

"What?"

"Look."

Two cargo loaders, in nice green uniforms, hurried across the runway toward us. The one on the right carried a large box.

"How can he run that fast carrying that thing?" I said.

"Strong," she said.

"Nobody's that strong."

She nodded to the man.

"Well, somebody is."

The other thing that looked odd was the dark glasses on the second cargo loader. Why would you need dark glasses at this time of day?

Betsy went back and opened the cargo door and stood there waiting for them.

Something about it all still struck me as wrong.

There were last minute cargo additions all the time. But this one . . .

I had just finished up the checkout, and was all ready for takeoff, when Betsy said, "Oh, shit."

"Beg pardon?"

"I said, 'Oh, shit.' "

"I heard you. What I want to know is *why* you said 'Oh, shit.' "

"Because there's a man here holding a stunner on me."

And then, of course, it all came clear: our guests were Sara Ford, the one carrying the huge box which was no doubt empty, and her blind daughter, who was no doubt the one in the dark glasses.

"What's going on now?" I said.

"He's tying me up," Betsy said.

"Actually, it's Sara Ford and her daughter."

"Who the hell," Betsy said, "is Sara Ford and her daughter?"

"Just shut up," Sara Ford commanded, "both of you, and right now." Then: "You go over there and sit down."

She was talking to her daughter. I noticed her harsh tone. To Sara Ford, revolutionary and zealot, all people were born to be ordered about. Even young, blind daughters.

She came up to the cabin and sat down in the copilot's seat and looked over at me.

It was a good plastmask. Must have taken twenty minutes, a half hour, to put on this skillfully.

She looked like a mean and not unduly bright guy who spent his time throwing cargo into skimmer holds and hating every minute of it.

"This thing ready to roll?" she asked.

"Ready."

"Then let's get going."

"You know if Betsy is out?"

"Just gave her a stunner shot on .05."

"I happen to like Betsy, and if you've hurt her in any way, I'm going to break your goddamned neck."

"I'm the one with the stunner, Duvall. You seem to forget that. Now get this crate rolling."

She started peeling off her plastmask.

In moments, I saw her outrageously beautiful face, albeit with tiny pink pieces of plastmask adhesive sticking to the jawline and cheeks.

"Get going," she said again. Then, back over her shoulder: "Take your plastmask off. And get my backpack out of the crate."

Again the harsh, almost military tone. No affection, no fondness for the blind daughter.

I was about to activate takeoff mode when the communicator said, "Duvall, please scrap takeoff and report to the tower."

McClure. No doubt about it. He'd figured out who the cargo loaders were.

"Get going."

"They said to scrap the—"

"Screw what they said. I'm the one with the stunner."

And to remind me of that, she pushed it into

my face. The alloy of the muzzle was cold against my temple.

"Get going," she demanded again.

There were three of them, McClure in the lead, and they came bursting out of the tower on the ground floor. They were heavily armed, and looked extremely unhappy. Extremely.

The stunner muzzle was once again applied to my temple.

I took off.

I put it full out. With somebody like Sara Ford, there was no chance of faking it, of going slow enough for McClure and his mini-posse to catch us.

She wanted to take off, and by God, that's just what we did.

We started down the runway with a blaze of lasers arcing blue and hot through the dusky morning air.

The blaze of lasers was meant to do us great bodily harm, but they were too late to do any real damage.

We lifted off with no problem, and in moments were streaking away.

"They'll come after us," I said.

"McClure isn't a pilot."

"No, but I'm sure he'll be able to find somebody there who'll take him up."

"It's barely five o'clock."

She was, as always, smug, and vaguely patronizing.

I got angry.

"Look, he's going to goddamned find somebody, and they're going to goddamned come after us, all right? McClure's a Federation agent and you don't get to be a Federation unless you're relentless, and relentless means coming after us as soon as possible." I glared at her. "Understand?"

She glared right back but said nothing.

I spent the next fifteen minutes concentrating on flying the ship.

All Sara Ford said every few minutes was, "Can't this thing go any faster?"

I knew what she was trying to do, of course. She wanted to get to the border of the Zone before McClure could catch up with us.

Federation agents fly over the Zone only in big, bad high-altitude Federation ships.

If a Federation agent gets shot down in the Zone, his death promises to be a slow, grim, and certain one.

We were fifteen minutes from the border, flying over land green with spring, when I felt the first hit, a laser ack-ack gun from maybe three or four miles behind us.

"That bastard," Sara Ford said.

"Mom, what was that?"

"Oh, for God's sake," Sara Ford said to her blind daughter, "can't you quit whining? I'm busy."

I turned around and looked at the sweet little girl.

"We'll be all right," I reassured her.

"Quit babying her," Sara said. "You're like my husband. That's why she turned out the way she did. All icky-sweet and scared of everything that moves."

The second shot came, and it was no ack-ack gun. It was two, no, three stiff volleys from a wing weapon.

The skimmer pitched right, then left.

Alloy smelled of burning.

"Mom! I'm scared!"

"Oh, for God's sake, Emily," Sara said.

The next volley came then.

This time the skimmer went into a slight dip.

Emily screamed.

I felt like screaming, too.

McClure's ship was hitting us hard and fast. There was a good chance he'd be able to knock us out of the sky before we reached the border

Then there was a good chance that we'd all end up in a Federation prison, even Betsy, who didn't have a damned thing to do with it, and Emily, who had the misfortune to be hatched from Sara Ford's cold, hard womb.

"Isn't there anything you can do?" Sara Ford shouted.

"Not really. I don't have any military weapons."

"And they do?"

"They sure do. McClure managed to find some kind of fighter. That's where the laser fire is coming from."

More fire, now.

I'd righted the skimmer, but now its nose dipped down once again, and the verdant land rolling beneath us suddenly seemed much closer. Forests look great until you think that you may be about to crash into them.

"How much farther to the border?" Sara Ford asked.

"A few miles."

"Then we can make it?"

"I'm not sure."

And, as if to make my point, another barrage of laser fire hit the tail section. This time, the tail didn't simply smoke, it caught fire.

The border appeared suddenly, the top section of the giant concrete wall that separated Federation from Zone.

Just a few more minutes, and we'd be there.

Sara Ford seemed to know what I was thinking the moment I eased up on the speed.

"No way," she said.

"No way what?"

"No way we crash on this side of the wall."

"You don't want to crash in the Zone?"

"We crash over here, McClure'll get me for sure."

"We crash in the Zone, and the cannibals may get us."

"There aren't any cannibals. That's all bullshit."

The stunner was put to my temple again.

"Max speed."

She'd kill me. Right there on the spot. Melt my head down and take over flying herself.

I didn't have any choice but to comply.

I gave the skimmer full power.

About a half mile before we reached the concrete fence, McClure let go with a smoke grenade that exploded on contact, and blinded my viewer completely.

The cabin started filling up fast with greasy, roiling smoke, too.

We were going to crash now, for sure.

"We'd better make it to the Zone," Sara Ford said, "or I'm going to waste your ass right on the spot."

Behind me, Emily was pleading for help, but of course her mother paid no attention.

We started going down then, following the path of the descending nose, the turbos screaming, the last of the laser blasts tearing the tail section off completely.

Down and down, we went.

I wasn't sure if we'd made it into the Zone or not.

After a few more seconds, I wasn't sure of anything at all.

PART TWO

1

This is what I learned later, and it certainly ended any fantasies I'd ever had about someday being a hero: soon after our skimmer crashed somewhere in the Zone, a terrible fire broke out on board.

Betsy, who had shaken the stunner's effect just moments before we crashed, was the only one conscious after impact. She managed not only to free herself, but to drag each of us, one at a time, to safety before the inevitable explosion sent pieces of the skimmer flying into the surrounding woods.

According to my chrono, I hit consciousness about twenty minutes after impact.

I was propped up against what the folks in Pennsylvania call a pin oak.

I knew I'd been cut at least slightly because the left side of my jumpsuit was soggy with blood, and I knew I'd banged my head pretty hard because pain was radiating from behind my ear all the way up to the crown of my head.

Even so, I had to acknowledge that it was a beautiful day.

People who've never been in the Zone imagine that it's a dark and somber place. They imagine that the countryside mutated along with some of the people.

I sat on the edge of a vast clearing.

On the west end was the smoldering remains of my skimmer.

But the rest of the clearing was green and lovely with buffalo grass, and it was surrounded on all sides by majestic trees that ran to sycamores and shagbark hickories and a few sugar maples.

The temperature felt as if it was in the low seventies. Sunlight was rich and warm.

I heard distant dogs, and an owl closer by, and no more than ten feet away sat a raccoon, as intrigued by me as I was by him.

Then I heard the crying, and turned to look on the other side of me.

Emily was propped up against a tree, too.

The left side of her face was scabby with dried blood. Her silver jumpsuit showed dirt and grease and smoke smudges. She seemed to have been hurt some.

Her very pretty face rested against her fragile hands as she sat there and wept.

There was no sign of either her mother or Betsy.

I started to crawl over to her, then stopped abruptly.

Lower back pain shot up my spine and into my neck. The crash had taken more of a toll than I'd realized.

I started crawling again, this time much more carefully. The pain wasn't so bad if the movement wasn't too fast or jerky.

A soft breeze came, rich with the minty scent of the forest around us, and dried my sweaty face. I wanted to roll over on my back like a family dog and let the breeze have at me.

Emily became aware of me suddenly because she stopped crying and took her hands from her face and brought her chin up a little and listened, the way blind people do when their radar indicates that somebody or something is incoming.

"Mom?"

"Afraid not, hon. It's Duvall."

"Oh."

"Did you get hurt pretty bad?"

"I hit my head. Mom really got nervous."

"About you hitting your head?"

"Uh-huh. That woman Betsy got us out."

Then she told me all about Betsy's heroics.

"That's why I hope Mom doesn't hurt her," she said.

"Why would she hurt her?"

"Well—"

She stopped talking.

I was afraid for Betsy suddenly.

"Do you know where they are?"

"Mom took Betsy's stunner from her. Betsy ran off. Mom went after her."

By now, I'd forgotten about my lower back pain. I managed to stand up on creaky legs. I also managed to discover that my stunner was still in its holster.

"Why would your mother want to hurt Betsy after Betsy saved her life?"

She had a lovely, earnest heart-shaped face. The dead blue eyes only added to the magnificent sorrow of her little face.

"I'd better not say. If I did, then you'd be in trouble, too."

"I have to find them," I said.

"I wish I could help you. I felt sorry for Betsy."

"Yeah," I said, thinking of how Sara Ford had cut down her husband. She'd have no problem cutting down Betsy.

"I'll have to leave you alone."

"That's all right. Anyway, the smells are beautiful."

"Yeah, they are."

"Is there an animal watching us?"

"Uh-huh. Probably more than one actually, but the one I can see is a raccoon."

She giggled.

"Raccoon. That's a funny name. Could you describe him?"

I wanted to get going, but I felt guilty about leaving the kid alone this way. Beautiful as it was, this was still the Zone and every kind of creature imaginable could be lurking in the shadow forest.

I described the raccoon.

She giggled even harder.

"He really has a mask?"

"Uh-huh. He looks like a burglar."

Then I heard the scream, faint, feminine.

"I've got to go, Emily."

I still felt guilty.

I bent down, pain shooting up my back as I did so, and said: "All you have to do is pull this trigger. It's set to go off."

"Is this a stunner?"

"Yeah, it is." I'd given her my spare stunner—the one I always carry strapped to my ankle—just in case.

"But how will I know where to point?"

"Point where your ears tell you to point."

"Mr. Duvall?"

"Yes?"

"I'm not like my mother."

I leaned down and kissed her on the cheek.

"Remember, all you have to do is point and pull the trigger."

She looked up at me with that earnest little face and said, "Point and pull the trigger. I guess I can manage that all right."

The scream had come from the west.

I took a trail through the sparsest part of the forest, one that wound through a low-lying tract of land that was still soggy from a recent rain. My feet went *twack* running through the puddles.

There were no more screams. None that I could hear, anyway.

I eventually came up on top of a limestone cliff, a ragged monument of Silurian bedrock that spoke of days when ancient bands of men, what kind we've never been sure, had roamed these lands.

Sara Ford was directly below me, skulking.

She was trying to get around a boulder, on the far side of which Betsy was crouching.

I drew my own stunner and decided to scare the hell out of Sara by burning off a big piece of the boulder she was presently traversing.

She didn't scare.

When the piece of rock chipped off, when the laser stench from my stunner was at its foulest, all she did was turn calmly around, locate me up on top of the cliff, and beam off a number 10 blast meant to melt me on the spot.

She found a smaller boulder, one that hid her pretty well from me, and started blasting away.

I had to find cover myself, and then return fire just to hold her down.

All the time I did this, I watched Betsy slowly climb up the big boulder, using only hands and feet for purchase, and eventually make it to the top.

She stood up there, Queen of the Mountain, for at least a full minute, obviously considering what to do next.

She could have jumped straight down on Sara Ford, but Sara was on the opposite side of the small boulder, too.

I don't suppose I would have minded killing Sara. The effects of her beauty had long worn off me. But Emily needed a mother, even one as treacherous as Sara.

When I looked at the big boulder again, Betsy was gone.

Sara fired off another blast at me, making me shrink down again behind the small copse of hickories.

Then Betsy was back atop the big boulder and hurling a rock down to where Sara crouched.

The ploy worked.

Sara, frightened, jumped up from cover, and spun to point her weapon in Betsy's direction.

But Betsy was ready for her.

She beamed a few seconds of Tranquil, the brilliant red beam instead of the standard blue, directly into Sara's chest, folding her over, knocking her out. As soon as I reached them, I retrieved Sara's stunner and stuck it in my pocket.

"God," Betsy said, "what a great bod she's got."

"Yours isn't so bad."

"Maybe not, but it's not in her league."

It seemed an odd conversation to have as we carried Sara—Betsy the feet, me the arms—to a nearby creek where we propped her up against a jack pine and waited the ten minutes for her to revive.

I knelt next to the water, played my hand in its cool clarity. I was thinking all sorts of idyllic fishing thoughts, until I realized that in the

Zone, creeks were probably one of the major toilet facilities.

I pulled my hand out and stuffed it into my pocket.

"What the hell made her so mad, anyway?" I said.

"What I saw."

"Yeah?"

"Yeah. That daughter of hers is a tel, and a damned talented one."

Tels are the most relentlessly pursued of all Undesirables. There has long been the rumor that the Federation captures tels and is presently training them to become part of a very special army that nobody could ever defeat.

"A piece of debris from the explosion was about to fall on her mother. Emily saw it and froze the debris right in midair."

"You're kidding."

"I guess I'd want that kind of thing kept a secret, too."

"I didn't think tels were that powerful."

The story the Federation always put forth was that telepathic powers were largely mythical, that all these ominous stories about tels were started by the Zoners to scare citizens. The bogeyman is coming to get you, and he's a tel.

"You know what Emily can do," I said. "You know how powerful she is. You saw her for yourself."

"God," Betsy said, "that's scary."

"Oh?"

"Of course. If she can do *that* with her mind, what else can she do?"

"Yeah," I said, "I guess that is kind of scary."

A few minutes later, Sara started moaning, reviving.

When I felt she wouldn't drown, I carried her over to the creek and threw her in.

She called me a lot of names as she climbed, shivering, out of the water.

2

Most folks don't die when their skimmers get shot down. The metal birds are built to absorb all kinds of punishment, and to provide a cocoon for the people inside.

The problem comes *after* the crash.

Then you're on your own, your only communication with Federation land being the beamers that send signals up to one of the satellites, then angle them back down to one of twenty-six Federation posts.

Even though my beam was picked up, and even though I was rescued, I have the sense that most beams get lost. Sort of like those signals being shot into deepest space on the off chance an alien species might pick them up.

Emily was safe, still propped against the tree, still holding the stunner.

Betsy and I went over and knelt down by her.

"I heard something once," Emily said. "I thought I might get to use the stunner the way you showed me."

I looked at Betsy and smiled. The kid was sorry

she hadn't gotten a chance to blast the hell out of something.

Then: "Is my mom here?"

Though we'd been back fifteen minutes, Sara Ford had yet to acknowledge her daughter in any way. She'd been going frantically through her backpack, and even after she'd pulled out a stunner to replace the one I'd confiscated while she'd been knocked out by the Tranquil, she continued to look for something.

"Emily would like to say hello," I said. "Why don't you come over here?"

"My daughter is none of your business," Sara Ford said, "and I'd appreciate it if you'd leave her alone. She likes to play on people's sympathies, and she's very good at it. Don't let her suck you in, Mr. Duvall."

I watched the little face, the blue blind eyes. A kind of wince, perhaps more a tic than anything, registered the pain from her mother's words. And then the tiny earnest face was still again.

I reached down and took the kid's left hand after I noticed that Betsy had already taken her right one.

"She doesn't mean to be like that," Emily said. "She's just worried about— Well, how things are going to go once we get to Los Angeles." A teeny frown: "I better not say any more."

"Shit," Sara Ford said after a minute, and hurled her backpack to the ground as if it were a bad dog that had just tried to bite her. "Where the hell is it?"

"Where the hell is what?" I said, walking over to her.

"None of your fucking business," she snapped. And then kicked her backpack with long-legged savagery.

"I have to go back to the skimmer," she said.

"I hate to tell you this, but there isn't any skimmer to go back to. Maybe you didn't notice that little fire we had."

"I don't give a damn about any fire. I'm going back to the skimmer."

"I'll go with you if you want."

She smirked. "And protect me with those big hard muscles of yours, Mr. Duvall?" She patted her holster, which now held her spare stunner. "I can do all right by myself." Then: "And don't get any ideas about my daughter."

"What the hell's that supposed to mean?"

"She's a beautiful little girl with a beautiful little body. Men are always sniffing around her."

"She's fourteen years old."

The smirk again. "You've never had sexual thoughts about fourteen-year-old girls, Mr. Duvall? I think about sleeping with fourteen-year-old boys all the time. They could give me a lot more pleasure than old bastards like you or my dear departed husband, that's for sure."

She hiked up her holster, patted it lovingly one more time, then walked over to Emily.

"I don't want to see you holding my daughter's hand ever again," Sara Ford said to Betsy.

She lashed out with a foot, breaking the hands apart.

"And as for you, young lady, I don't want you playing all your bullshit sympathy games with these people, understand me? 'Poor little me' and 'Big Bad Mommy.' I'm tired of it, Emily. You need to grow up and quit making people feel sorry for you."

She turned back to Betsy. "You probably have something better to do besides sitting here with my daughter, don't you?"

And with that, she left the clearing, heading back in the direction of the skimmer remains.

I followed her anyway.

I stayed a tenth of a mile behind, her on the trail, me in the undergrowth.

The last time I'd been stranded in the Zone, I'd picked up a minor but irritating case of poison ivy on my hands. I was careful this time.

When we neared the clearing, I selected a tree that looked relatively easy to climb, and started up.

It was a pin oak, and there was one thick branch especially good for spying. At the moment, it was occupied by a mother squirrel and two baby squirrels. The mother and I exchanged looks.

I eased myself a few feet out on the branch and stopped as soon as the mother squirrel turned around to glare at me.

She was not going to abandon the branch to me; but she would share it if I went no farther.

I went no farther.

The first half hour, the crash site still smoldering about thirty yards ahead of me, down there on the grassy ground where Sara Ford was grubbing through the smoking debris, I mostly spent looking around the countryside.

To the north were red clay cliffs ragged and rugged and beautiful against the cloudless blue sky.

To the south was heavy timberland that ran half a mile down to a narrow muddy river.

To the east was a valley. It had been mostly farmland once but now the fields lay fallow.

To the west rolled small hills covered with jack pine, a hawk diving and rolling and soaring above the ragged pine peaks as if putting on a fantastic show for all the small forest creatures below, big Disney eyes peering up from the shadowy woods.

I didn't know what the hell she was looking for, and after a time I wondered if she did either.

Mostly what she did was curse things and kick things as she scavenged among the pieces of still smoking skimmer.

One time she kicked out and missed her target, and drove her foot into a tree. The cursing, I imagined, could be heard for miles.

All this went on for over an hour. I had to shift position several times to keep my cheeks from falling asleep, and each time I moved, mother squirrel shot me a threatening glance. Like any good mother, she expected me to sit there and be absolutely still.

She never found what she was looking for, or if she did, she found and pocketed it so quickly that I didn't see it.

She was standing, hands on hips, cursing in a low voice, when the thing burst from the trees on the far side of her.

The thing made her scream, and I liked that. I'd never seen Sara Ford be vulnerable to anything and it was a pleasant experience.

The thing came close enough to her to make her back up and draw her stunner.

She was just raising the weapon, and sighting down its long alloy barrel, when I saw the thing's face and realized that it was some form of human, of what humans had once been, anyway or, God forbid, might be in the future.

He looked like some kind of throwback, all stoop shoulders and wide, flat face, and hairy body. The third eye, a lifeless blue orb in the middle of his forehead, was what made him really remarkable, of course. He held a crude knife in one hand and a rock in the other as he came up to Sara Ford. The man wore boots and jeans but no shirt. He was probably a good five feet and a half, or would have been if he'd walked straight upright.

Even from here I could see the grief in the two quick, dark intelligent eyes. He said something, or tried to, and whatever it was, it was more plaintive than frightening.

All of this was lost on Sara Ford.

She had now pointed her weapon directly at the man's chest and was about to pull the trigger.

I had my own stunner out now and fired two quick shots at her gun wrist, knocking her stunner to the ground and forcing her to grab her gun hand in great quick pain, the way bad guys always do in the Old Western holos I watch sometimes.

She forgot all about our three-eyed friend for a moment and looked up at the oak branch, shrieking and cursing as soon as she saw it was me.

The man looked up, too.

There was no gratitude in his expression, just bafflement that somebody had saved his life.

But he wasn't still for long.

From the forest behind him, along the path the man had used a few minutes earlier, came a mob of perhaps a dozen men, all of them carrying weapons that ran mostly to clubs, spears, and knives.

The three-eyed man was gone.

I hadn't seen him go.

I'd been too busy watching the small mob.

And then there were shouts from the opposite side of the clearing where the skimmer had crashed, and the three-eyed man was in sight again.

Two men, big and rough, and looking very much like the others in the mob, came pushing out through the trees, with the hairy man struggling to get free of their grasp.

They threw him in the center of the clearing, near where Sara Ford stood uncharacteristically silent.

And then, once again reminding me of one of those Old West holos, one man in the mob produced a rope and ran over to a nearby tree and tossed the rope over the lowest and sturdiest branch he could find.

Lynching was what they had called it in the Old West.

The three-eyed man was really struggling now, seeing the quick and final fate awaiting him.

"Kill the bastard!" one man shouted.

A man on a horse appeared on the edge of the clearing. He saw what was going on and then walked his horse over to the mob and dismounted.

He gave the reins of the horse to one of the two men fixing up the rope.

Now they had everything they needed to kill the three-eyed man.

He was on his knees now, directly below where the hangman's noose swung in the soft breezy afternoon, and he was crazed with fear, sobbing and pleading in a way I'd never heard anybody sob or plead before, grunts and cries that were not quite human.

I was about to see something very, very ugly.

3

I didn't have much choice.

As the mob encircled the three-eyed man, I fired my stunner near the edge of the group. I used a very low beam but it was still enough to rip up a good chunk of earth and to put the stench of laser burn on the air.

To a man, they all turned to glance around at the nearby woods.

I helped them by walking out on the tree branch so they could get a better look at me.

The mother squirrel glared at me some more. I stopped within two feet of her.

"I'm up here," I said to the mob, "and I have a stunner and if you try to hang that man, I'll kill all of you. Do you understand?"

I was looking around at them when I realized that Sara Ford had disappeared.

"All right," I said, "where's the woman?"

They said nothing, just stared up at me, hands filled with their weapons, eyes filled with their fury.

Each of them, when you looked carefully, had

some sort of mutation or deformity, an outsize ear, or ratlike teeth, or oddly glowing eyes.

But for the Zone, these men were the Normals.

The wretched three-eyed man was one of the real mutants, and he was obviously paying for it.

"Where's the woman?" I said.

She screamed.

I had my answer.

She was somewhere in the shadowy forest, and not far away at all.

Even the mob turned to see where the scream had come from. They saw her before I did, and their bearded, dirty faces broke into homely smiles.

A very big guy, six-nine or so and maybe three hundred pounds, flung Sara Ford out of the forest.

She landed in a heap on the ground.

Her cursing was sharp and vile.

But the big guy didn't care.

He just stood there in his bib overalls and checkered shirt and Western-style straw hat ogling the stunner he'd taken from her.

Like a child with a toy he doesn't quite know how to use, the big guy slipped his finger across the trigger and turned toward me before I understood what he was doing.

I'd let his size and the bib overalls convince me that he wasn't any too bright.

But he was bright enough to aim the stunner directly at me, and bright enough to set afire the branch that I, and the squirrel family, occupied.

The limb ripped away from the tree with a terrible cracking sound.

The mother squirrel screeched and chittered angrily. I had the stray thought that I should apologize to her in some way. I'd grown to like her and wanted to protect her.

But then I was smashing against the ground, and gripping my stunner so it wouldn't get away from me, and I couldn't protect anybody, not even myself.

The earth was solid; my flesh and bones were not.

The impact was enough to give me stars for a few moments, and to send pain radiating up my entire right side.

Then a boot the size of an anvil was crushing my wrist and a hand ripped the stunner from my fingers.

I looked up to see the big guy smiling down at me. He had no teeth and the wispy little beard he was trying to grow was pathetic. But I thought I'd better wait till later to give him my opinion of his beard. Just in case he was sensitive on the subject.

The rest of it happened pretty fast.

I was grabbed and dragged over to another oak tree.

They lashed Sara Ford and me to the tree and then stood back to admire their new captives.

"Who the hell are you?" demanded the big guy.

"Who the hell are you?" I said.

I tried to sound as belligerent as possible, to make him think that I was in control, not him. The quaver in my voice didn't help.

"My name's Lem, asshole, and I work for Alison."

"For whom?"

"Alison, jerk-off. The woman who runs this whole sector of the Zone."

He was winning in the belligerence sweepstakes.

For one thing, he was a lot bigger than I was. For another, he wasn't nearly as stupid as I'd guessed at first. And for a final point, he held both stunners.

Maybe Lem was going to expand his territorial holdings and very soon.

There couldn't have been many stunners floating around in the Zone. Possessing one could make a weak man strong. And a strong man, like Lem here, a whole lot stronger.

"Our skimmer was shot down," I said.

Not till then had I noticed how tightly they'd tied us up.

The circulation was already gone in my hands. Soon it would be gone in my feet, just below where the rope cinched my ankles.

"Zoners shoot you down?"

I shook my head.

"Federation," I said.

"Federation shot you down? You're not a Normal?"

"We're Normals. Both of us. But the woman—she's in the Front."

I figured mention of the Front might buy us some sympathy. Here was a group—well, all right, a *mob*—of Zoners doomed to spend their lives out here living like animals. It was the intention of the Front to integrate them into Normal society so that Undesirables, too, would enjoy the fruits of education, medicine, and indoor plumbing.

But mention of the Front had seemed to have the opposite effect.

Anger filled Lem's blue eyes suddenly.

I wasn't sure what he was angry about, just that he was starting to grip those stunners awful hard.

"She's part of the Front, huh?" Lem said, and then walked to the other side of the tree to face Sara Ford.

"Thanks a lot, Duvall, you asshole," she said to me as Lem came around to her.

He hacked up a good goober and spat in her face.

The sound of him getting the goober up was bad enough.

Hearing him spit was even worse.

Sara Ford was apparently so shocked by what he'd done that she didn't even curse at him.

"I hate the Front," Lem said. "I hope the Federation kills every one of you sons of bitches, you understand me, girlie?"

He walked away from the tree, and over to

where two men were keeping the three-eyed man on the ground at gunpoint.

He'd stopped bleating, the three-eyed man, and now sat Indian-legged with his hands over his face, as if he were trying to will everybody away.

Lem walked over to him, raised a booted foot, and drove it deep into the three-eyed man's ribs.

The three-eyed man's hands came away from his face. He looked at Lem and said, "Please don't do that no more."

"You lyin' little bastard," Lem said.

The three-eyed man shrugged.

The men didn't waste any time keeping Lem happy. The rope was once again tossed over the branch, the hangman's knot brought into proper position, and the lone horse set under the knot so the hanging would be fast and clean.

Another man went over and drove a boot into the three-eyed man's ribs just as Lem had.

"Rather kill him with my hands than hang him," he said as the three-eyed man doubled over again.

The pecking order was clear.

The closer you were to Normal, the more power you had.

If you looked like the three-eyed man, you didn't have any power at all.

There used to be black, self-hating African nations like that. The more white the hue of your skin, the more privileges you enjoyed.

Watching them get everything ready for the

hanging, I also had a good notion of why Lem here hated Federation people so much.

If integration ever came, Lem and all the other Lems in the Zone would lose their power.

In the Zone, Lem was one of several kings.

In the world at large, he wasn't even a joke.

They got the three-eyed man to his feet.

He started bleating again.

There wasn't anything else to call it.

It was a noise both sad and comic, both chilling and embarrassing.

You rarely heard people exposing themselves with such uninhibited force.

The front of his jeans were stained.

He'd peed his pants.

They got him over to the horse, and though he started kicking out at them, they managed to get him up into the saddle, and then they managed to get the noose around his neck.

He started so violently in the saddle, with the noose dropping down around his neck, that the horse spooked momentarily, and bucked.

The lynch party scooted away from the frenzied horse.

The three-eyed man would have been pitched off the saddle if the hangrope hadn't been holding him in place.

The chestnut mare calmed down.

The men returned to setting up the lynching.

The three-eyed man seemed out of energy suddenly. He slumped forward in the saddle, his eyes closed.

He didn't seem to care anymore. He'd pretty much accepted what they were going to do to him.

He was saying something under his breath. I had a good idea he was saying prayers of some kind.

"You men about ready?" Lem bellowed from several yards away. He sounded angry.

"We sure are," the man nearest the chestnut mare said.

"Then hang the sonofabitch," Lem said, "and hang him now, and hang him good. You understand me?"

The men nodded.

"Then slap that sonofabitchin' horse, and let 'er go."

That's all it would take.

One slap across the horse's backside, and the animal would jerk to a start.

He'd run fast enough to slide out from under the three-eyed man in seconds, leaving the man to dangle there and choke to death.

"You don't be too concerned with him," Lem shouted at me. " 'Cause right after we're done with him, it's your turn. And then the gal's."

Lem grinned.

"I sure hope that's a strong rope," he said. "I sure do."

That's when the gunfire in the woods started, and that's when everything got real confusing and real dangerous.

4

Lem had a stunner in each hand. Theoretically, this would make him invincible against five people with shotguns and handguns.

The trouble was, for all his bluster, Lem wasn't especially gifted with the stunner.

Five people came out of the woods, armed and firing, and all Lem managed to do was chop down a couple of trees and put one hell of a scorch across the rocky face of a boulder. The stunner isn't easy to aim.

Meanwhile, the folks coming out of the woods killed four or five of Lem's men in an ear-numbing shootout.

The new gang was led by a short, plump woman in a Western shirt, jeans, and boots. Her gray hair was pulled back behind her angular head with a festive blue ribbon. She had one of those sweet, smart faces that made you think of grandmothers and cookie baking.

But there was nothing domestic about the way she wielded her Winchester, or about the way she advanced on Lem's gang with no show of fear at all.

She must have killed two or three of them herself.

Not until she got closer to the tree where Sara Ford and I were tied up did I notice the silver star on the front of her Western shirt.

A badge.

A Western sheriff's badge.

She was about ten feet from me when Lem, in a burst of genius, figured out how to work the stunner.

He set the degree up high, aimed it at one of the sheriff's men, and put a sizzling hole the size of a basketball in his midsection.

The sheriff didn't flinch. She just turned back to the woods and said, "Bring Vince out!"

At the mention of Vince, Lem's eyes narrowed, he looked at the part of the woods where the sheriff had shouted, and the stunners fell silent in his hands.

I didn't have to wonder who Vince was.

He was as big as his brother Lem. The only difference was his shock of red hair. He even wore the same kind of bib overalls.

Two men held Vince at bay with shotguns.

"They'll kill me, Lem."

He sounded scared.

"You want to see him dead, Lem?" the sheriff asked.

"Where the hell'd you find him?" Lem replied. "I been lookin' for him for two days."

"I found him over at Overton's still," the sheriff said.

"Overton told me he wasn't there," Lem said, sounding hurt.

"Hell, he lied to you. He lies to everybody. I just went up to the second story of his house and there was Vince. I knew I'd need him. I heard you were gonna try and lynch Potter here, and I figured your brother was the only leverage I'd have to stop you."

"Potter's a mutie," Lem said. "And he's a carrier."

Later, I was to learn that some muties were believed to carry a few plague germs—but this had never been proven. Of course, this didn't stop people from lynching them, true or not.

"He needs to be tested, not lynched. That's the only chance we got in the Zone, Lem. Law and order. We live like animals out here, Lem. It's time we stopped."

"You'll just let Potter go."

"We'll let him go if he's not carrying anything."

He brought the stunners up again, aiming them directly at the sheriff.

"You see what I done to that deputy of yours. Look at his stomach."

It was pretty impressive in its grisly way, the work the stunner had done.

The kid lay sprawled on his back, arms flung wide. The hole in his middle, broiled flesh, had attracted a variety of inquisitive forest creatures, including a red fox that got close enough to the corpse to get itself covered in big, black, noisy flies.

"If you don't untie those two people and give them back their stunners, Lem, I'm going to personally kill your brother right here and right now."

Lem smirked. "I thought you wanted all this law and order."

"I do, Lem, but sometimes you have to take extreme measures to accomplish things. I wouldn't mind killing Vince anyway, Lem, to be perfectly honest. He's killed twenty, thirty people over the last couple of years, and he's killed most of them in front of witnesses, too. A lot of them were defenseless women." She raised her Winchester and pointed it directly at Vince's head.

"I wouldn't mind if you killed me, Lem," the sheriff said rationally and calmly, "since I know I'd have time to take your bully brother here along with me. You understand?"

Lem looked down at his stunners and then back up at the sheriff.

"You let him go, then?"

"Nope. We're keepin' him locked up until the medical tests are over. If you're good, and don't interfere with things, you'll get him back when the tests are all over."

"Shit, Mae, this ain't fair."

"Maybe it isn't, Lem. But the mood I'm in, I don't much give a damn."

The three-eyed man made whimpering sounds of gratitude.

This was probably the first time in his wretched life that anybody had ever defended him.

Mae pushed the muzzle of her Winchester directly against Vince's head.

"She'll kill me, Lem. She really will," Vince said.

"This really pisses me off, Mae," Lem said.

"Put down the stunners, Lem. And right now.

"Really, *really* pisses me off, Mae."

But he put down the stunners.

One at a time.

And with great reluctance.

But he set them down on the grass.

And Mae eased over and picked them up.

"You know something, Lem?" she said, when she had both stunners tucked inside her wide leather belt.

"What?"

"I was almost hopin' you wouldn't hand them over."

"You was? How come?"

"Because I would have enjoyed killing Vince. All the women he's beaten and killed in these parts. It just makes me sick to think of. It really does."

She nodded to the tree where we were tied.

"Now cut them free. I'm taking them back to the settlement with me."

Mae didn't cut me or Sara Ford a hell of a lot of slack. I wondered why. I'd gotten the impression that she wanted to protect us from Lem. Now I wondered who was going to protect us from her.

She kept our stunners stuffed in her belt, and kept her deputies right on our backs with their shotguns and rifles.

We went back through the long grasses and the edge of the forest. Lem and his gang had drifted off in the opposite direction.

"You running contraband?" she said to me at one point.

"You mean guns?"

"Yeah, that's just what I mean."

"Huh-uh."

"Just a poor innocent guy flying over who got shot down by Zoners, huh?" She wasn't going to believe my story even if it was the truth.

"You people are sure making it hard for people like me," Mae said, walking next to me.

Sara Ford had fallen back.

The two men guarding her positively glowed every time she looked at them.

Lovestruck, I thought.

Wait till they got to know her a little better.

"What 'people' you got in mind?" I said.

"Hell, let's quit playing games, all right? You've been running guns back in here and you had an accident and now you're trapped."

"You see any guns at the crash sight?"

She shrugged.

"No big deal there. No reason the guns wouldn't have survived the crash. The guy you were selling them to just took them away. How many cases you bring in this trip?"

"I'm not a gunrunner."

"Right."

She nodded to the three-eyed man who walked on ahead of us.

"That poor guy," Mae said. "The only chance he's got to survive in the Zone is if we have law and order. My grandparents and my parents worked all their lives to bring it to the Zone, and they died tryin'."

"How'd they die?"

"People like Lem."

"Oh."

There was a bluebird, and then a jay, and then a wren, all sitting merrily on tree branches watching us as we walked beneath them.

"Lem has a lot of power out here. His kind of power. Law and order came along, he wouldn't be half as important as he is now. He's above the law, and that's the way he wants to keep it."

"You think he's buying guns?"

"No doubt about it. There're five gangs out in this piece of territory, and Lem's is the strongest because of the weapons he's got."

"You ever catch him at it?"

She smiled. "Not yet. But my luck may be changing real soon now. Real soon."

"For what it's worth, Mae, I'm not a gunrunner."

She eyed me with great professional suspicion.

"You know, I'm starting to believe you. At least a little bit."

Coming from her, I took that as a high compliment.

When we got back to the clearing, Betsy and Emily were gone.

Sara Ford went into a panic.

"Where the hell did they go?" she said over and over as we started searching the countryside.

Her maternal concern surprised me. I wasn't convinced it was maternal concern, anyway. Sara did things only for herself, not other people.

The day was dying. The shadows in the woods were deeper. I smelled pine and mint and wet, black earth. I stuck to the path. I didn't want to get lost.

Fifteen minutes later, I came out into another smaller, wilder clearing, this one with wild bunch grasses hip-high. The clearing ran down to another creek, and by the creek, propped up against a tree, I saw them.

Betsy sat on the ground, her back to a tree. She was asleep. Emily was asleep, too, with her head on Betsy's shoulder.

I wanted a picture of them.

I'd never seen Betsy so peaceful-looking, nor seen the frightened Emily look so safe and secure.

I touched Betsy's shoulder.

Her eyes came open lazily, fluttering beautifully like a princess' in a Disney holo, and at first she didn't seem to recognize me, just took me in with her soft gorgeous eyes.

"You got a lot of people looking for you, kiddo. Emily's mother is on the warpath."

Betsy yawned.

"We just fell asleep, I guess."

Emily stirred, now.

She yawned, too.

She reached out and touched my hand tentatively.

I took her soft little hand and held it.

"Your mom wants to see you."

"See, I told you, Betsy," Emily said.

Betsy smiled, stood up, then helped Emily to her feet.

Betsy said, "We went looking for butterflies. I described everything I saw. We were having a great time but—"

"—but I told Betsy that my mom would be mad if she came back and I wasn't there."

"So it's all my fault," Betsy said. "I'll explain that to Sara."

"I wish I could stay with you," Emily said. "I wish you were my mom, Betsy."

"C'mon, Emily. Your mom's worried about you."

"No, she's not. Not in the way *you* mean, anyway." Even though her remark was obscure, it gave me the impression that I'd been right. Sara's concern hadn't been maternal at all. She was worried about Emily for her own reasons.

We started back.

Emily said, "I love this time of day. The smells are richer."

"It is beautiful," Betsy said.

"I'm going to ask my mother if I can stay with you again tomorrow, Betsy."

Betsy and I glanced at each other.

It was pretty obvious why the kid didn't want to stay with her mother. But, after all, Sara was her real mother and had certain rights.

I doubted that even cold, stony Sara would just hand over her daughter to anybody.

Especially since, as I sensed, there was something she needed from Emily.

We walked on, and as we walked, I became aware of Betsy very near to me.

Whatever I'd once felt for her was back, and I didn't like it at all.

Loving somebody who doesn't love you is a pain in the butt for both parties.

You moon around all the time, and spoil everybody's fun, including your own.

She caught me looking at her that way, and smiled.

"Maybe we can find a campfire to sit around tonight, Duvall."

I tried not to read anything into that. So I changed the subject.

"Yeah, if we don't get lynched first."

"Lynched?"

I told her about Lem and the three-eyed man and then all about the sheriff named Mae.

"That's where we're going now, the little town she runs?"

"That's what she says. And we can't argue with her. She's got our stunners."

"You think they'll have food there, in her little town, I mean?" Emily said.

"They'll have some kind of food there. But I wouldn't bet on what kind."

"Fried alligator, maybe," Betsy said.

"Issh," Emily said.

"I was joking," Betsy said.

"Good, because I was getting sick just thinking about it," Emily said.

When she saw us, Sara didn't come running out to throw her arms around her daughter.

She simply said: "And just where the hell were you, young lady?"

"It's all my fault," Betsy said.

"You, I'll talk to later. Right now, I want to talk to my daughter."

"But, Mom, all we did was—"

Sara was there, then, grabbing Emily by the arm and dragging her off toward the forest.

"The poor kid," Betsy said.

"Yeah."

"She makes me want to have kids."

"I thought you *never* wanted to have kids."

"Well," she said, "with the pilot and all, I guess I started thinking about having a family."

"You wanted *his* kids?"

"I didn't really know what he was like at the time."

She had tears in her eyes and I could see I'd pushed her too hard. The pain of him was still fresh in her.

"I'm sorry, Betsy. You'd make a great mom."

"You really think so?"

"Uh-huh."

"I really shouldn't have been so stupid about him, should I have, Duvall?"

"Well, we're all stupid about somebody."

She smiled tearily.

"Yeah, I guess we are."

"I was stupid about you," I said.

She looked at me carefully.

"But you're not any more, huh?"

"Nope. Not any more."

"Even if I came to my senses and changed my mind about you?"

I resented her a little bit then, couldn't help it. I just didn't want her to know how I really felt. Pride, I suppose.

"Even if you came to your senses and changed your mind about me," I said.

She looked at me some more.

"You really mean that, Duvall?"

"Yeah," I said, "yeah, I do."

Then I went off to look for Mae.

5

Mae called it the Settlement.

What it was, or had been once, was a very small housing development, little ticky-tacks as people called them back then, each looking pretty much like the other, each with a minimum number of architectural flourishes and safety requirements.

We arrived just after dusk.

There being no electricity, lamplights were set up between the houses. Inside the windows, you could see the flicker of candles and kerosene lamps.

The houses at the head of the Settlement had been converted into other things. One announced GENERAL STORE; a Christian cross stood atop another, indicating a church; LIBRARY decaled a third; and RECREATION boasted a fourth. SHERIFF'S OFFICE was down the line a ways

Around the perimeter of the Settlement, heavily armed men and women patrolled with dogs so lean and savage you almost hated to look at them. They'd mutated somehow, the dogs, and bore almost no resemblance to the big, floppy, smelly pooches who'd sit in your lap and make you feel better when you were down.

Sara Ford was next to me as we reached the Settlement. I watched her take it all in. It was like watching a computer take inventory of a large warehouse. Every item properly categorized for future use. Sara, beautiful as she was, scared me a lot more than the guard dogs did.

As we walked down the main street, which was a wide dirt path wetted to keep the dust down, people of various ages peered out their windows at us.

I don't suppose folks here got visitors very often. Little kids looked at us, and grandmothers, regular dogs and regular cats looked at us, too. And moms and dads and uncles and aunts also, all watching, watching, watching the strangers.

There was a melancholy about it, the croupy coughs of little kids and a woman weeping softly somewhere and the faraway screams of older children playing until their mothers absolutely made them come in; and a sadness about the sky, too, the dying day turning slowly to purple-streaked dusk, and the first stars just now starting to shine indifferently above us.

Many of the people in the windows called to Mae, and you could hear affection and admiration and the need for approval in their voices. Mae was pretty clearly the most important person in the Settlement.

She found a house for us on the west end of the Settlement.

We weren't carrying much equipment, so settling in was pretty easy.

There was a living room and two bedrooms and a bathroom and a kitchen.

Mae gave Sara and Emily the bedroom with the single bed, and Betsy and me the room with the twin beds.

Soon as she left the room, Betsy said, "She doesn't trust us." And laughed softly.

And then she slid her arm around my waist and we just stood there for a time like that, the early stars shining against the darkening sky.

"This is all pretty crazy."

"Yeah, it is."

"What's going to happen to us?"

"I don't know."

"Can you keep a secret?"

"Uh-huh."

"If I ever get the chance, I'm going to steal Emily."

"I know what you mean."

"Sara is such a bitch, I can't believe it. She nearly knocked her down twice today."

"I noticed."

She held me a little tighter. Her hair smelled good. Her body was warm and tender. I wanted to hold her tighter, too. But I stopped myself. I don't have a high tolerance for pain. I'd get all het up again and she'd meet some other dreamboat, and there I'd be again.

"I'm sorry about the way I used to treat you, Duvall."

"It's all right."

"No, it isn't."

"How about shutting up?"

She laughed, and then we just stood there like that some more, and this time I couldn't help it. I closed my eyes and held her tight and dreamed the old dreams.

"Young love," Sara Ford said from the doorway. "How touching."

She came into the room and said, "I want both of you to leave my daughter alone. You understand me? You've got her very confused right now, and I can't afford to have her confused." The only light in the room was starlight. Curiously, the way it etched her face in shadow, it made her look ugly. There was something reassuring about that.

"You understand me?"

"Yeah," I said, "we understand you."

"And that goes for you, too, sweet lips."

"I have a name," Betsy said.

"Yes, but it isn't one I'd care to use in polite company."

And with that, Sara Ford left us.

Dinner was stew served in two steaming bowls.

Betsy and I ate together in our room.

Betsy said, "I wonder what this stuff is."

"We're probably better off not knowing."

"You serious?"

"Hell, yes, I'm serious. What if it's something like rat or prairie dog?"

She spat a mouthful of the stuff back into her bowl.

"God, Duvall, why'd you have to go and ruin my dinner?"

"I was just using an example."

"You really think this could be something like that?"

"Look. We crashed in the Zone. There aren't any four-star restaurants out here."

"But who could eat a rat?"

"You could if you were hard up enough."

She stared down into her bowl.

We had a kerosene lamp now. The golden light of it made her freckled face seem more kidlike than ever.

"You know what I'm watching for?"

"What?"

"Watching for anything that moves."

"I'm sure it's all right."

"I'm serious. Stare at yours for a while. See if anything moves."

I stared.

"Oh, God," I said.

"What?" she said, earnestly.

"I see two rats down there. They're in a rowboat."

"You asshole."

"Betsy, it's fine. Watch me. I'm going to take a

big spoonful and put it in my mouth and swallow it."

I opened my mouth and shoved in a spoonful and swallowed it but all the time I kept thinking about rats.

Not the ones in the rowboats I'd pretended to see but the ones that might have been trapped and skinned and then tossed in a stew pot.

I didn't feel real good.

She said, "You're thinking about rats, aren't you?"

"No."

"Yeah, you are. You looked sick when you swallowed that stuff. And it's just what you deserve."

"You're not going to finish yours?"

"Just the bread."

"I'll ask Mae about the stew."

"If it's rats," Betsy said, "I don't want to know."

There was a kind of town meeting that night, a good number of adults assembling in an open patch of grass on the edge of the Settlement.

Mae presided.

I stood back in the shadows, watching and listening. What they were doing, these people, was divvying up communal chores. This man would cut the Settlement grass, this man would lay in wood for next winter, this woman would have sentry duty six nights next week, this woman would train the older children in martial arts. And so on.

They sat there in a semicircle, fanned out around Mae, the torchlight gleaming on their faces, raising hands and making their points with complete civility. I couldn't ever remember seeing people who were as respectful of each other as these folks.

The meeting lasted just over half an hour.

When it was done, they stood up and took their turns greeting Mae personally. It was like a receiving line.

When they turned back to the Settlement and their homes, they looked at me with interest, but no hostility. Mae had introduced me at the top of the meeting. She said that I was from the Federation and that my skimmer had crashed. There'd been no questions directed at me. They were much more interested in their own lives. They'd had enough of a glimpse of us when we'd trekked down their main street a few hours earlier.

"Where's your friend?" Mae said when she came up to me.

"Betsy?"

She nodded.

"She's working on trying to jury-rig a beamer from scrap."

"She must be a good technician."

"A lot better than I am. But that's not saying much."

A lantern swung from Mae's right hand,

casting a golden nimbus against the woodsy darkness all around us. There were fireflies, and the scent of apple blossoms. I wanted Betsy alongside me.

"If she's got something worth working with in the morning, I'll see if we can find Rupe."

"Rupe?"

"Rupert Goldman. He's one of the brains from Sutton Village. That's a settlement a little farther downriver. Bunch of people who used to be university professors all live there with their families. They've got the biggest library of any settlement in the whole Zone. Rupe taught engineering. He's handy with just about anything you care to name."

"He doesn't charge you?"

"Oh, no. We barter. We usually give him things we pick up from scavenging. We found an old lawn mower and he went crazy. He always says it's his favorite thing next to his wife and kids. Anyway, Rupe usually travels on Tuesdays and Wednesdays. When he gets done here, he goes west and stops where the farmers have a settlement. He fixes things for them and then he tells them what kind of food his settlement needs. The farmers deliver it for him a few days later. Same with the Mall Settlement."

"What's that?"

"Big shopping mall used to be just off one of the old interstates. Whole village sprang up there about ten years ago. Kind of like a swap shop. You can trade and barter. The folks have the stores all fixed up and open again and they found an old ferris wheel for the kids and Rupe's good at keeping the motor running and all."

I laughed. "You've got a whole civilization out here."

She stopped at an old limestone well, set her lantern on the edge, took a coin from her pocket, and dropped it down the well.

"My mister always did this every night we'd go for a walk together."

Her voice was thick with sentiment.

The coin dropped; long seconds later, I heard a tiny echoing splash.

"He was quite a guy. Been gone eight years now and I still miss him." She sighed. "Lem's friend Alison, one of her men killed him. Murdered him in cold blood. Frank saw a young girl being raped and tried to stop it. And died for his trouble. I found the man who killed him and got him in a fair fight and shot him three times in the chest. But it's Alison I really need to kill. If it wasn't for her, this Settlement of ours wouldn't need so many people on patrol every night."

She looked back down in the well. "Frank always made the same wish. That we'd all be happy here. That's the kind of guy he was. Always thinking of other people."

She was crying, so I slid my arm around her shoulder and she pressed her damp face against my chest and held me for a brief time.

"Thanks. I appreciate it."

"Any time."

We started walking again.

"I guess I don't know who Alison is," I said.

"She's the warlord."

"The warlord?"

"Every outlaw gang in this part of the Territory has to pay her part of what they take. Or she'll kill off a good part of their gang. She's got her own settlement up the river. And she's got an army of about two thousand men and women. That's who buys all the guns from the gun-runners. There's a skimmer landing in her settlement a couple of times a week. She gives them drugs to sell, and they bring her weapons, mostly rifles and grenades. But that's all you need to run things out here—if you've got a couple of thousand people to back you up, anyway."

I laughed. "I just can't get over the name."

"Alison?"

"Yeah. It's kind of a cream puff name for a warlord, isn't it? I mean, Genghis Khan and Attila the Hun and—Alison."

"I see what you mean."

"Alison the Conqueror."

"Believe me. She's no cream puff. She's real pretty in a tough kind of way. But she's also crazy. They hang two or three people a day in that settlement of hers. And a lot of the time they cut them up like sides of beef and let them hang there for days until the vultures are done with them."

She nodded to the Settlement houses as we approached.

"A lot of the people who live here now used to run with Alison. But I tried to show them that it wasn't any way to raise kids. They figured that just because they're uneducated and weren't wanted by some of the other settlements, they had to live like animals. But they've come a long way. You saw them tonight."

"I was impressed."

"No reason for people to live the way Alison wants them to," Mae said. "There's a lot better alternative."

She yawned.

"I'll take you over to the Island tomorrow."

"The Island?"

"I want you to see how the real mutants suffer out here. I want you to go back and tell your Federation friends about what you see."

For the first time, there was a hint of bitterness in her voice.

"I'm sorry, Duvall. I get all worked up when I think about what those poor people on the Island have to go through."

We walked a few more yards in silence.

"This is my place," she said, indicating a small gray tract house.

She yawned again.

"We can take Betsy, too, if you like."

"I'll ask her."

"She looks like marriage material, Duvall."

"Yeah, she does."

"Out here, when a man sees marriage material, he does the sensible thing."

"Marry her?'

"Yep. And right away."

"I'm not sure she'd want me."

"Then she's a fool."

"Would you mind pointing that out to her?"

Mae laughed.

"You think that'd help?"

"Couldn't hurt." I shrugged. "I think she likes men who're a little more dashing than I am."

Mae shook her head.

"I knew a 'dashing' man once. Took me for every cent I had and then ran off with my fourth cousin Sue. You tell her if she wants to know anything about dashing, come and talk to old Mae. Now you go get some sleep, Duvall. After all you've been through, you need it."

No way I was going to argue with that.

Every time Mae had yawned, I could feel sleep tugging my eyes closed.

I said good night and walked back to the house.

6

Betsy was asleep when I got back. I tried to tiptoe around, but she woke up anyway.

In the darkness, I found my cot and lay down. I was tired.

"I had a bad dream," she said.

"Yeah? About what?"

"This guy I used to see."

"Oh."

"What's that supposed to mean?"

"What's what supposed to mean?"

"The way you said 'Oh?' "

"I didn't know I said it in any particular way."

"Right."

"I didn't."

"I know you don't approve of me, Duvall."

"Oh, shit, I'm too tired for this tonight." We'd gone around about this a few times before.

"You think I've been with too many men."

"Your past is your business."

"Yeah, right."

"It is."

"That's a crock and you know it."

I sighed. "I could use some sleep, Betsy."

"So could I."

"Then why don't you shut up?"

"Why don't *you* shut up? In fact why don't you shut the *fuck* up."

I knew better than to say anything.

Then, "I'm not a whore, Duvall."

"I know you're not."

"I've been with some men but probably not as many as you think."

I didn't say anything.

"How many *do* you think I've been with Duvall?"

"Maybe a hundred."

"You asshole, are you serious?"

"Okay. Maybe twenty."

"Sixteen, if you want to know. How many women have you been with?"

I counted them up. It wasn't difficult.

"Four."

"Really? Four?"

"I never claimed to be a womanizer."

"That's kind of sweet. Four."

She yawned.

"I'm getting sleepy."

"So am I."

"Why don't we kiss each other good night and go to sleep?"

We kissed.

When she was lying on her bed and I was lying on mine, she said, "That was really sweet, Duvall."

A minute later, she was snoring.

* * *

I had a dream about the beamer.

It's strange, the things you dream about sometime.

The beamer was lying in the woods, over near an oak, lost in some deep bunch grass. The impact of the crash had hurled it there.

I found the beamer and down came a Federation rescue ship—which is just about the most hazardous duty you can find anyway, being on a Federation rescue crew—and then suddenly the dream shifted to this improbably large and improbably fine reception area in the back of the ship . . . and I was standing before one of those robopreachers . . . and Betsy was standing next to me . . . and we were getting married.

When I woke up, I half-expected Betsy to be lying next to me. I also half-expected to be in a very posh honeymoon hotel suite.

What I got was the hard cot and the scratchy blanket I'd been sleeping on. As for Betsy, she lay on her cot, left arm flung off the bed, snoring.

Moonlight shone through a jagged piece of shattered glass.

I sat up on the edge of the bed, rubbing my face. Once I was awake, getting back to sleep would be difficult. I decided to check out the crash site again. Maybe, as in the dream, I'd find the beamer.

The guards gave me odd stares as I walked past them. I waved to show that I was friendly, but I decided against explaining myself. This wasn't a prison. Or I hoped it wasn't, anyway.

The night was ridiculously gorgeous. Rain had perfumed the entire forest and now the blooms of a dozen wildflowers filled the night air. The stars were almost unnaturally bright, so my path to the woods was easy.

I heard nightbirds and coyotes and wild dogs; I heard homeless cats and thrashing raccoons and splashing otters from down in the creek.

Even if I didn't find the beamer, the walk would be worth it. This was the dream I'd always had for my wife and daughter, living someplace like this, someplace where they could be relatively safe. But we'd never quite had the money. Personal freedom is expensive these days.

In the moonlight, the wrecked skimmer resembled a piece of metal sculpture, all twisted and burned out. It would need a dramatic title. OBLIVION, or something like that.

If I ever got back safely this time, I'd have to borrow the money to buy another skimmer. This one had come from my savings. I'd have to go to a cargo company and hire on as one of their pilots. They'd take a large percentage of my salary and apply it to the purchase of the skimmer I flew.

The crash site still smelled of oil and smoke.

I took out my shiner and shone it around all the obvious nooks and crannies, just in case I might have overlooked something earlier, and then I started shining it around in not-so-obvious places—down the hill, behind the larger rocks, in a small patch of clover.

Nothing.

I decided to start on the west side of the hill and work all the way down to the creek.

I don't know how long I was looking before I heard them. But by the time I *did* hear them, it was way too late.

There were two of them and they came up over the hill about the time I reached the creek. They were on horseback.

I turned to face them.

They both trained rifles on me.

I reached for my stunner, then remembered that Mae still had it.

The tall, blond one said, "You stay right where you are."

"And he ain't whistlin' Dixie," said the small, swarthy one.

They wore a kind of prison uniform, blue work shirts and denim pants. Their carbines were old-fashioned Winchesters.

They ground-tied their animals and came down the hill.

"Where's the girl?" the blond one said.

"What girl?" I said, though I assumed he was referring to Emily.

"What girl, my ass. Where is she?"

The blond one had a peach stubble beard. Up close, he didn't look any older than twenty. He could have used a shower.

"One of our people seen what she done, and

they came back and told Alison, and she said to go get the girl." This was the dark-haired one, and he was very matter-of-fact about it all.

"Girl like her would bring a good price from the Federation," the blond one said.

"You deal with the Federation?" I said, surprised.

The two glanced at each other.

Obviously, the blond one had said something he shouldn't have.

The dark one cocked his carbine and put the muzzle against the tip of my nose.

"So where is she?"

"I don't know."

He grinned, the dark one did.

"I think I just found me something to do tonight, Merle. I'm gonna take this sonofabitch apart."

"Take it easy, Clancy," Merle, the blond one, said. "He won't do us any good dead."

"Well, he sure ain't doin' us much good alive either."

That's when he shoved the butt of the Winchester into my solar plexus.

I dropped to my knees.

He kicked me in the ribs.

I fell over frontward.

He came over and stepped on my hand with the sharp edge of his boot heel.

"Now where is she?" Clancy said, putting all his weight on my hand.

"She's right here, you dumb bastard."

All I could raise were my eyes. Right now lifting my entire head would have been too much trouble.

Betsy came down the side of the hill. Somehow, she'd managed to get my stunner back from Mae.

"You two boys have any idea what this is?" she said, pointing the stunner at them directly.

They glanced at each other and nodded.

"Stunner," Clancy said.

"Uh-huh," Betsy said, "and I'm going to use it on you if you don't go over there right now and pick him up and dust him off. You understand?"

The two looked at each other again, then came over and got me to my feet.

At first, I thought my hand might be broken. But after a quick examination, all I could feel was a bruise.

"Now get back to your horses," she ordered.

"Bitch," said Clancy as he walked past her.

"Dickhead," Betsy said in reply.

"Slut," Merle said.

"Asshole," Betsy said.

They got on their horses up there on the crest of the hill, the moonlight turning their mounts silver, and started slowly away.

"You all right?" Betsy asked.

"I'll live. How'd you get my stunner?" I questioned.

"Mae was asleep. I snuck into her room."

"How'd you know where I was?"

"I followed you."

"But why?"

"I just wanted to see where you were going. By the way, where *were* you going?"

"Looking for the beamer," I said.

"Oh."

"Let's start back. I'll look for the beamer tomorrow."

"Yeah," she said, "I'm tired." Then: "They know about Emily."

"Yeah."

"We've got to keep a close eye on her."

We walked back slowly, enjoying the rich night air and the lonely stars and the orchestra of the forest animals.

"You mind if I change my mind?" she said as we drew near the settlement.

"About what?"

"About not wanting anything to happen."

"Ah."

"If I change my mind and want something to happen, Duvall, will you change *your* mind and want something to happen?"

"I guess I'd have to take that under consideration."

"For how long."

"Oh, upwards of ten, fifteen seconds."

She laughed.

And right after that, I kissed her.

We went back to our little house, and this time something happened.

7

The bugle blast caused me to jerk awake and sit up straight. I pulled a good part of the scratchy blanket with me, leaving Betsy nearly nude and struggling to wake up.

"God," she said, "what's that awful noise?"

"Bugle."

"Bugle?"

"Apparently that's how Mae wakes everybody up around here. It's sort of like an old-fashioned army base."

I got up and struggled into my clothes and went over to the window to watch the Settlement come to life.

People of all ages, sizes, shapes, colors, and temperaments started streaming out of their doorways and walking to the center of the Settlement where a communal breakfast was being served. Beef was being cooked, and eggs grilled, and bread toasted. The only odor missing was bracing dark coffee.

"Am I hallucinating, or is somebody fixing

breakfast?" Betsy asked as she climbed into her jumpsuit.

"It's for real."

She came over to the window and stood close to me.

"Aren't they cute?"

She referred to two small sisters, maybe four or five years old, holding hands as they left their parents' house and walked to the breakfast line.

"I never realized how much you liked kids before."

"Just because I don't wear a flowery little dress doesn't mean I'm not maternal."

"I'd like to see you in a flowery little dress sometime."

She said, quite seriously, "Last night, I had a great time. But I don't want to mislead you again."

"We had a nice time. Nothing less, nothing more."

"Damn, Duvall, why'd you go and let me fall for that bastard anyway?"

I smiled. "So now it's my fault, huh?"

She slid her arm around me and said, "I've got to blame somebody, don't I?"

I went through the breakfast line twice. I would have gone through three times, but I didn't want people to guess that beneath my human exterior, I'm actually a hog.

Many of the people ate quickly, and got to their jobs. Some headed for the fields to farm, some were building the school Mae had pointed out, some took groups of kids to the red barn now being used as a school, some went to work in the white barn where everything from bread to rope was made, and at least a couple of dozen headed for the small hills with their rifles. Apparently, this was the military unit to be used against Alison. There were more women than men, and the ranges seemed to run from teenage up to the early sixties. The Settlement was alive.

We found a table way in back to sit, away from the Settlement people. While they didn't look unfriendly, they didn't exactly looked charmed by us, either.

I was well into my second helping when I saw Sara Ford and Emily appear. Emily got everybody's attention. A small blind child so beautiful was not somebody you saw very often.

Sara brought Emily to our table and sat her down without a word. Then she went to get their breakfasts.

"Did you get some sleep?" Betsy asked her.

"A little. But I was scared."

"Of what?" I said.

Emily shrugged fragile shoulders. "I just kept thinking about those men who were going to hang the man with three eyes."

"How do you know he had three eyes?" Betsy said.

"My mother told me."

"Oh," Betsy said.

"She said that Alison is just as bad as real Federation people. They all hate anybody who's different from them. That's why my mother wants to kill them."

I started to laugh, but Betsy shook her head.

I wanted to point out that wanting to kill people because they disagreed with you was just as bad as wanting to kill people because they didn't look like you. It's why I couldn't ally myself with either side in this war. They were both fanatics.

Emily reached across the table and found Betsy's hand. "I'm glad to be with you again."

"Me, too, honey."

"Last night I was wishing—"

Then she stopped herself.

"Well, I was just thinking of how my life would be different if you were my mother instead of Sara."

I wondered what Betsy was going to say in response but she didn't get a chance to say anything, because Sara set down two plates steaming with breakfast.

"Have they been teaching you some more about peace and tolerance, Emily?" Sara smiled. But it was clear she wasn't joking.

"No, we've been talking about how my life would be different if Betsy was my mom instead of you."

Sara, ever lovely, held off putting a forkful of scrambled egg into her mouth.

"Well, isn't that sweet?" Sara said. "I wonder if Betsy would have been willing to go through all the childbirth problems I had with you. And then drag you around like a god-damned ball and chain all the time. It's not real easy being a hand-maiden for a blind person, sweetie, no matter what you might think."

I watched Emily's sweet little face. In the clear morning light, her freckles were infinitely more numerous and colorful. She had a perfect little nose and a perfect little mouth. The perfect little useless eyes were now filling up with tears.

"I guess I shouldn't have said that," Emily said, "about Betsy being my mom."

"Remember what I've taught you, dear. Any time you hurt me, I'm going to hurt you right back. You understand?"

"Well," Betsy said, before the scene got any more angry or painful. "You feel like a morning stroll?"

"I sure do."

"I can see that you don't approve of how I'm raising my daughter," Sara Ford said. "But I don't want her to turn into some bourgeois hypo-crite. She has to know that when she strikes somebody, then that somebody is going to strike back."

I knew it wasn't my place to say that maybe Emily wouldn't lash out if Sara ever showed her even a moment's warmth. But it wasn't my place.

" 'Bye, Emily," I said. "We'll see you later this morning."

We spent the morning walking around the Settlement. There were two churches, one for believers and one for agnostics; there was a martial arts class for older children, and a shooting range for teenagers and up; and there was a basement where a lot of artwork was displayed, some of it pretty good, all of it done by people here at the Settlement. People raked, painted, cleaned, pounded nails, worked on roofs, doors, chimneys, windows. There were white faces and black faces and yellow faces and red faces. Everybody seemed to get along just fine.

Just before lunch, we ended up at Mae's. You'd think, with her being in charge and all, that her place would be grand or at least remarkable in some aspect. But it wasn't. It was just this little aqua-colored tract house with three words stenciled neatly on the wall next to the door:

Constable
Judge
Arbiter

Mae came to the door and said, "You can come in, but be quiet, all right?"

The living room was set up with a massive oak desk and some folding chairs. A gavel sat on the desk and a black judicial robe hung from a clothes tree.

In the next room, which had formerly been the dining room, were two seven-foot cages with heavy locks latching them shut. This was the jail. There was another jail out back where Vince and Potter were being kept.

We veered sharply to the right, down a long narrow hall.

At midpoint, a door stood ajar. I peeked in and found that this was Mae's place. The walls were covered with dozens of photographs of a young, good-looking Mae with a young, good-looking man, her husband. There was a single bed with a festive pink comforter on it, and a rocking chair, and a bookcase bulging with titles, and a viola standing upright in a corner. The place was cozy and warm, a safe haven.

The bedroom farther down the hall was different. There was a small table and two chairs. A young man of maybe twenty sat at the table. He was pale and sweaty and watched us with guilty blue eyes. He had straw-colored blond hair and had a raw, hungry look, like a street urchin. Somebody had put handcuffs on him.

"This is Vic," Mae said, as she brought us into the room. "He was just about to tell me when the next Federation ship picks up dreamdust from Alison."

As we'd learned this morning, a lot of Federation people were involved in pushing drugs. If the Federation and the Zone were ever reunited, there would go their profitable business. If you took the dreamdust out of the picture, the Federation people would have less reason to fight the Zone being integrated as part of the country again.

Vic was pale and sweaty. A couple of times, he looked as if he might lean over and barf.

"Vic made the mistake of sampling the merchandise," Mae said. "Now he's a dreamduster himself." There was no anger in her voice, just sorrow.

She put her hands flat on the desk and leaned over and put her face right into his.

"When does the Federation ship land, Vic?"

He was scared. "They'll know it was me who told you, Mae."

"You'll be safe here. As long as you don't leave."

"Yeah, but I won't have any—"

She sighed.

"You won't have any dreamdust."

"Right," he said. "I'm real sick, Mae. I really need some."

Dreamdust comes from the silphium flower. It's illegal to grow on Federation land, but Alison grew and refined it by the ton.

Mae stood up straight.

"We raid as many fields as we can," she said to us. "We can't stop it all, but over a six-month period, we can do some damage. Or we could. About four months ago somebody started telling Alison in advance where we were going to raid next. This one was going to be the biggest of all. We were going to raid one of her refining factories." She sighed. "When we got there, they were waiting for us. Killed six of our people."

She nodded to Vic.

"But what are a few lives when Alison keeps Vic in dreamdust?"

"I didn't mean for no people to die, Mae."

"But they did die, Vic."

He was crying now, coming apart. Most of it was his need for dreamdust. But there was probably some remorse in there, too. He looked like a kid who'd made some bad miscalculations, and who suddenly woke up to find himself the principal player in a nightmare.

"I'll do anything you ask, Mae."

"No, you won't. I asked you when the next Federation ship lands, and you said you didn't know."

"I'm not lying to you, Mae."

"Sure you are, Vic."

He screamed and clutched his stomach as best he could with the handcuffs on. Then he fell out of the chair and started flailing his legs. At first, I thought he might be faking. But then he started vomiting, and I knew better.

Mae ran from the room and said, "Be right back."

Betsy and I went over and knelt by the kid.

Betsy put her hand on his head. It was amazing. The kid quit flailing at once and lay still now, breath coming out of him in hot ragged bursts.

She soothed him like a healer, stroking his forehead gently, slowly.

He looked up at her with those guilty blue eyes and said, "I really fucked up, didn't I?"

"Yeah," she said, "you did. But you want to know how many times I've fucked up?" She smiled. "Hundreds of times. And you know who's really a fuck-up?"

"Who?"

"This guy right here."

I wasn't sure I wanted to be used as an example of screwing up one's life, but at the moment I didn't think I should argue about it.

"You really got in trouble before?" the kid said.

"Lots," I said.

"Bad trouble?" he said.

"Terrible trouble."

"And you came out all right?"

"The handsome, successful multimillionaire I am today."

"I got some people killed. I didn't mean to."

He started crying again.

This time, Betsy began stroking his cheeks, wiping off his tears.

Mae was in the room again. She had a hypodermic needle and a piece of cotton that smelled of alcohol.

We stood up so that she could kneel down next to him.

"This is going to put you out for a while, Vic," Mae said. "Right now, you need sleep more than anything."

"I'm sorry I got those people killed, Mae."

"I know, Vic."

"I didn't mean to."

"I know that, too, Vic."

She swabbed his arm with the cotton and then quickly put the needle into his arm.

"I'm sorry, Mae," the kid said again, and then he was gone.

We carried him into Mae's room and laid him out on the bed. She put a blanket over him.

"What's going to happen to him?" Betsy said.

"There'll be a trial. A jury of six will decide."

"What happens if they find him guilty?" Betsy said.

Mae stared at the kid a long moment then shook her head. "He gets his choice. Either we execute him or we turn him free. Wandering around the Zone with a dreamdust habit is a lot worse than being executed, believe me. The last one like this, we found the carcass a week later. Pack of wild dogs had gotten him after he went into a coma. There wasn't a lot left."

A bitter smile touched her mouth. "If you think this is depressing, wait till you see the Island."

"Gee," Betsy said, "I can't wait."

8

I hadn't been on the water for years. I'd forgotten the pleasant smell of the water and inviting look of the shoreline on either side, sandy beaches and stands of white birch and pine, and the sense of centuries passing here. The shore probably looked pretty much the same three centuries ago when the first French trappers arrived.

There were several small islands in this stretch of river. The one we wanted, the main island, was still half a mile away as we roared down the river in the big outboard rig that Mae drove like a race driver. A couple of times Betsy looked over at me and rolled her eyes.

When we reached the shore, I helped Mae drag the boat up on the sand.

We were confronted by a long wall of birch trees growing very close together.

"Where's the hospital?" Betsy asked.

"About a half mile straight in," Mae said.

We started walking, the scent of pine cones strong on the soft breezes. I thought of pirates putting ashore on an island like this. Pirates had always fascinated me. If I had two lives, I would spend the second one looking for buried treasure.

Halfway there, the forest thinned out and we passed through two clearings. In one, we saw a moose. He just watched us curiously, standing perfectly still so we'd know he wasn't afraid of us. In the other clearing, we saw two young deer drinking from a narrow creek. Unlike the moose, our presence did bother them. They took off running in that gracefully awkward manner they have.

We climbed a very long hill and from the crest of it, we saw the hospital.

At one time, this had obviously been an antebellum mansion, complete with soaring pillars and a second-story veranda that had probably been perfect for sipping mint juleps.

"There it is," Mae said.

"God, it's beautiful," Betsy said.

And she was right. Even though the building needed some paint, and some work done on the roofing, and maybe a quick pass at the external shutters, the place had a majesty and mystery that was fun to contemplate, the embodiment of a more elegant era long passed. More elegant, that is, if you didn't happen to be born black, and a slave.

Mae looked through a pair of field glasses she had slung around her neck.

"If you look to the right of the house, you

can see some of them in the backyard," she
said.

She took the glasses off and handed them
to me.

I didn't really want to look.

Deformity always depresses me because it
proves how random all life is. A roll of the
genetic dice. If there does happen to be a god
behind all this, then he's got a pretty cruel sense
of humor.

They were more heartbreaking than I'd
ever imagined, tiny people, elephantine people,
people with no arms, people with three arms,
people who had bones sticking out of their
skulls, people who had eyeballs on their shoulders, people who were essentially ball-like,
people who looked hydrocephalic and did little
more than drool and twitch.

As always, I was stunned by it, overwhelmed
to the point that I was immobilized.

When I took the glasses from my eyes, Betsy
said, "You're making a real funny noise in your
chest, Duvall."

"Yeah, I probably am."

All I could think of was my wife and daughter,
and the lives they'd led. They were luckier than
these people in that they could pass . . . but their
fate was the same.

"You think you're up to it?" Mae said as Betsy
looked through the glasses.

"I guess so," I said.

Mae stared at me a moment. "You've got the wrong face."

"I'm not sure what you mean."

"You've got a tough guy's face. Hard eyes, broken nose, kind of a sneer on your mouth sometimes. But inside—"

I smiled. "Inside I'm a regular poet, huh?"

"This stuff gets to you. Far as I'm concerned, Duvall, that's a good sign for your soul. You can make fun of me all you want."

I'd hurt her feelings. "Thanks, Mae, for saying that. I just feel my status as a real macho guy is threatened whenever anybody calls me sensitive or anything like it."

"My husband was like that," she said, "a dope."

I laughed.

After Betsy handed the glasses back, she said, "Who takes care of them?"

"We take shifts at the Settlement. Everybody works over here about two weeks out of the year. Just the way they take turns serving in our militia."

"That's great," Betsy said.

"Well, they're our sons and daughters and grandchildren. It's only right that we'd help them out." Then: "Say, I meant to ask you, Duvall. How come you didn't bring Sara Ford and her daughter along?"

Betsy answered. "We're not getting along very well. Sara feels that we poke our noses into her parenting."

Mae grinned. "It's high time somebody did. That poor little Emily. What a sweetheart."

She pointed down the hill with a walking stick she'd brought along.

"Well, we might as well get going," she said

9

The iron gates had rusted long ago. Patches of the sprawling lawn had gone unmowed, as if parts had been selectively overlooked. There were stone fountains and stone benches set all over the grounds. The mutants looked at us with sad curiosity, as if they were gauging our responses to how they looked.

As we'd seen from the hill, every kind of deformity imaginable was on display here. There was even a kind of Siamese twins, a girl and boy joined in such a way that they could move about, the girl smiling at us, the boy glowering.

Some of the mutants hung back behind the edges of the mansion, and clung to the deepest shadows they could find.

Others, particularly the young ones, came up to us and held out frail hands.

When we touched their hands, they smiled, as if we'd accepted them despite their appearance.

All of them knew and apparently loved Mae.

She seemed to be a kind of celebrity to them.

She kissed the young ones on the forehead, and embraced many of the older ones.

We walked all the way around the mansion, greeting people.

There was a creek in back, a fairly wide one, and on the other side of this was a two-story brick house. Cyclone fencing ran all around it. Near the only entrance hung a sign:

PLAGUE

I was going to ask about it, but Mae was too busy with a new group of children.

These were special kids, I gathered. All six of them wore identical red shirts. One of them carried a huge accordion.

"They'd like to play some songs for us," Mae said.

"Great," Betsy said.

Their deformities ranged from having no nose and ears, to having heads shaped like pineapples.

But they were very good singers.

I stood there in the breeze, listening to them sing. I had both my arms and all my fingers and toes, and my ears and nose were in the proper place. I was filled with the kind of sorrow I usually felt only late at night.

Life really was random, a roll of the dice.

I could easily have been any one of these children.

It served no special purpose for my wife and daughter to be born Undesirable.

The accordion player did two solos and he was damned good. There's a merry sound to the instrument that no other can quite duplicate. I remember my wife saying that of all the dances, the polka looked like the most fun. We'd never quite gotten around to learning it.

After the entertainment, Mae took us into the house. The place smelled of medicine, cooked food, perfume, and age. The furnishings were a polyglot of styles, shapes, and eras, all harmonious in a strange and kind of shabby way.

Mae introduced us to a woman named Dr. Helen Reynolds, a thin, fortyish, intense-looking woman whose blue eyes belied her otherwise grave face.

Dr. Reynolds, in turn, led us through the mansion, up and down, twenty-two rooms in all. Essentially, the first floor was a hospital where people were operated on, and recovered.

Upstairs, the rooms had been converted into a kind of dormitory. Everybody had a bed and bureau. Forty-one people stayed here now.

Always, we were followed by little ones. Their deformities were the worst to see. I was just glad they were here and not on Federation territory. Teenagers would have hanged them on sight.

Back downstairs, walking toward the back door, Dr. Reynolds, officious in her white medical smock, said, "We've been very lucky this year. Very few mutants among the children born. In fact, mutations seem to have been trailing off for the past three or four years. We're not sure what this means. We don't really have the kind of laboratory equipment to make any kind of serious scientific study."

She walked out on the back porch and pointed to the house on the creek.

Mae said, "Some very interesting things are going on over there, Duvall. Why don't you tell them, Dr. Reynolds?"

The first thing Dr. Reynolds explained was how Plaguers were collected and taken to the house over there. If you showed persistent symptoms for a week, you were put in a quarantine shelter about a mile west of the Settlement. Many people got only a mild case of the Plague and, believe it or not, it often went away.

But not always.

If the symptoms persisted for three more weeks, you were taken to the house in back of the mansion, where you were monitored every day. Of the people brought to the house, roughly fifty percent developed a serious case of the flu.

"That's incredible," Betsy said.

"It sure is," I said.

"People in the Federation get just a few symptoms and they're dead almost right away."

"But over here—"

Dr. Reynolds smiled for the very first time. Now her sensual lips were as friendly as her blue eyes.

"We think we're right on the verge of explaining that," the doctor said. "A few more weeks and we may be able to understand it. We first noticed this five years ago. Now maybe we'll be able to understand what's causing the effects of the Plague to lessen. We're doing something right—but we don't know what it is yet."

Just then a man came from the quarantine house across the creek and ran to the gate and started rattling the lock, trying to open it.

From out of the house came a man in one of the camouflage militia uniforms.

By now, the man at the fence was frantic. He was screaming "I want out! Let me out!" and pulling on the fence so hard, I thought that he might pull it down.

He sensed somebody approaching and took off running. A second militia man came racing out of the house and also gave chase. The frantic man did some pretty impressive broken field running. Neither of the militia men could catch him at first. They ran in a broad pantomime of a chase, like an old-fashioned silent film, legs and arms swinging wide, expressions of dismay on the faces of the men pursuing, an expression of terror on the face of the man chased.

They even went all the way around the house, disappearing for at least a long minute, then reappeared again running faster than ever.

One of the militia men broke away and started running much faster, closing the gap between the frantic man and himself.

The frantic man panicked then, and inexplicably ran back to the fence. He started climbing the fence, and doing a very bad job of it.

The militia man didn't have any trouble jumping up and pulling the frantic man down.

They both tumbled to the ground. The frantic man got up first and started to turn and run away.

The militia man came up behind him and gently took his shoulder. The militia man said something to the frantic man and then started leading him back to the quarantine house.

By now, the man was no longer frantic. He was weeping. He put up no fight at all, just let the militia man steer him back to the house.

"That's Ralph, the patient, I mean," Dr. Reynolds said. "He's one of the people we haven't figured out yet. He and his family were all quarantined at the same time. But within three weeks of being put in the quarantine house, the wife and the kids were fine. And they were able to leave. But not Ralph. He still has some symptoms."

A little boy with a head not much larger than a grapefruit appeared on the porch and said, in a whispery voice, "Dr. Reynolds, they need you upstairs."

"Thanks, John."

The little boy stared a long moment at Betsy. He was obviously entranced by her sweet good looks.

Seeing this Betsy bent over and kissed him on the forehead.

He blushed, and went away.

Dr. Reynolds gave us her second smile for the day.

"Thank you," she said to Betsy. "He'll remember that for a long time."

Mae took us out to the front grounds again and we had our last look at the mutants. By now, the shock of it all was fading. As I looked, I saw not the deformities but the personalities. Some looked reasonably happy, some sad, some off in their own fantasy worlds.

A number of them clung to Betsy. It was more than her good looks, I think. They seemed to sense that she was a good woman, and that her goodness was worth their touches and admiration.

They followed Mae, too, all the way to the rusted front gate, their laughter trailing her like bright flowers.

"Don't they just break your heart?" Betsy said as we turned to leave. On the way back, she had to borrow my handkerchief three times.

10

The gunshots echoed off the hills, giving their bark a real ferocity. The shots reverberated off the high cliffs of red clay and then off the half mile of birch trees. This happened within moments of dragging the boat up on the shore of the Settlement.

"What the hell is that?" Mae said.

"Why don't you give me your field glasses?" I said.

I climbed a large oak, tearing hell out of my hands as I did so. Several more shots cracked on the air.

I got the glasses adjusted and took a look.

At the far end of the main street, I saw three bodies sprawled in the dust.

And a little farther away, three large, fierce horses galloping away.

On one of the horses was Emily, struggling to free herself from the arm of a black-uniformed soldier. On the second horse, kicking and elbowing her assailant in the ribs, was Sara Ford.

The raiders rode away fast.

I came back down the tree and told Betsy and Mae what had happened.

We hurried back to the Settlement.

11

They'd given up everything they were doing, the men and women and children of the Settlement, to see what the gunfire and the screaming had been about.

They stood in little clusters, watching in disbelief and shock and outrage as the three bloody bodies of their militia men were put on stretchers and taken to the two-story white house with the big red cross on it.

They'd probably convinced themselves, over a period of time, that they'd built themselves a little piece of civilization here in the Settlement. Oh, maybe not quite as safe or snug as their old civilization, but good enough to get by on.

But the killing of the three guards had shown them otherwise, had demonstrated that their hold on civilization was not nearly as strong as they'd imagined.

So they mourned, each in his way. The women tended to cry and the men to curse, though there were also men who cried and women who cursed. The children mostly looked dazed, not quite understanding what was going on here, and why their folks looked so upset.

Mae was quickly caught up in policing the killings, dispatching militia people here and there, doubling the guard, organizing a group of men and women to form a posse that would leave on horseback in an hour. They synchronized their watches.

The worst of Mae's job was to comfort the families of the two men and one woman who'd been killed. Not that she didn't have a natural capacity for soothing people—but it was hard to soothe when your own face was grim with anger.

Betsy said, "I wonder how Emily's doing."

"I'd like to go to the house where they stayed."

"For what?"

"See what Sara Ford left behind. Maybe we can find out why she was in such a hurry to get to L.A."

"Yeah, I guess that would be interesting to know, wouldn't it? Besides, it'd give me something to do besides stand here and worry about Emily."

As we walked toward the house, Betsy said, "So you think they took Emily because they found out she was a telepath?"

"Sure. They can sell her to the Federation for a lot of money."

There had long been a rumor that the Federation was collecting every telepath they could find and putting them in a special school in the Sierra Mountains. The rumor extended to the Federation creating a corps of telepaths that would basically run all the cities after the Federation declared a permanent state of martial law. They wanted to find every single Undesirable and kill him. In the old days, the Federation had simply been power mad. Now they were a lot more dangerous. They'd begun to believe that some higher power had instructed them to take over the entire North American continent.

There was a smear of blood on the small concrete front porch. A few drops stood red and bright on the threshold.

We went inside.

There'd been quite a struggle. Most of the smaller pieces of furniture—two end tables, a lamp, a small table for bric-a-brac—had been turned over or smashed. There was more blood spattered across the living room wall.

We followed a trail of smashed furniture to the back of the house, and the bedroom where Emily and her mother had spent the night.

A bedroom window had been shattered. One of the raiders had probably broken it, so he could get his gun trained on the sleeping women. The others probably came in through the front door.

The cot on the left side of the room had blood at the head and pieces of broken glass in the middle.

We started searching the room—closet, bureau, under the cots—but found nothing.

We checked out the rest of the house, spending twenty minutes upending furniture, opening and closing closet doors, even searching through the kitchen cupboards.

Zero.

"Maybe we should try the bedroom again," I said.

"We already tried the bedroom."

"I know. But that's where they probably spent most of their time last night, so that's probably where she would have left her personal things."

"If she had any personal things."

"Right," I said.

"I mean, I don't remember her bringing anything on board except her stunner and backpack, do you?"

I made a quick mental snapshot of Sara and Emily in the back of the skimmer. I took it from several angles. Betsy was right. All I could remember Sara having was the stunner and backpack.

"I still want to try the bedroom one more time," I said.

We went back through every single step we'd taken previously, just in case we'd overlooked something.

But we hadn't.

Zero again.

There was a knock on the front door and Mae's voice called out, "Betsy and Duvall, are you in there?"

"Yes," I answered. "C'mon back."

A minute later, Mae stood in the bedroom with us.

"I just wanted to tell you about the posse."

"Ready to go?" I said.

She nodded.

"Have either of you ever been on a horse before?"

Betsy and I shook our heads.

"Then maybe you won't want to go."

"We're going, no matter what," Betsy said. "I want to get Emily back."

"Same for you?" Mae asked me.

"Absolutely."

"Well, c'mon down to the corral, then. I'll try and find two horses that won't give you too much trouble."

Then Mae added: "Oh. I found this out in the yard. Maybe Sara dropped it when they were dragging her away."

She reached in her back pocket and took out several pages that had been folded together and handed them to me.

"I'm going back to the corral. I'll see you down there in a few minutes."

"Thanks, Mae," I said.

She swatted her butt. "Just expect to have a real sore backside for a long time," she said.

"Even with a saddle?" Betsy said.

"Even with a saddle, honey."

After Mae left, we went over to the window for better light and started going through the pages Mae had found.

At first, they didn't make much sense.

There were two pages torn from a magazine about nuclear missile sites.

"Who Controls These Missiles Controls The World" by Calvin M. Knox

The article talked about the different types of atomic weapons installations that had been used in America since the end of World War II. Knox speculated where these facilities were located, and which ones were launch sties. Then he listed all the things that could go wrong with such a site, and how easily it could fall into the wrong hands.

In several places, Knox mentioned Los Angeles, and how the U.S. Army had secretly created a launch site less than sixty miles outside Los Angeles County.

Sara, or somebody, had circled every mention of Los Angeles.

The third and fourth pages looked as if they had been torn from a paperback book.

"Telekinesis: Fact or Fancy?" by Ivar Jorgensen, Ph.D.

The ability to move objects through mind power has long been a controversial subject. Even the ancient Egyptians believed that certain human beings were endowed with this ability, particularly members of certain royal bloodlines. There was even a legend that one of the pharaohs, displeased with his accommodations in his pyramid, rose from his grave and moved great stones so that his followers were forced to rebuild the pyramid the way he wanted.

Most of the article dealt with the Russian experiments into telekinesis. According to Dr. Jorgensen, Russian parapsychologists had spent two decades researching telekinesis with some of their most gifted psi students.

The experiments were miserable failures. At first. A number of the students even died from no discernible cause. But gradually, two of their very best students began moving things.

One girl, Nadia H., was able to sit in one room and move a large mahogany table across the floor in the room adjacent to her.

A male, Sergei B., was able to lock and unlock doors with his mental powers.

Unfortunately, just as the experiments were beginning to break important new ground, there was a purge and the Communists, who had taken power once again, believed that all such experiments were "frivolous and decadent."

In the margin was written an address I didn't take time to study.

The final page was another from a magazine.

"Los Angeles After Nuclear Attack: A chilling speculation" by Richard K. Shaver

What you saw was what you got with this one—how Los Angeles would disintegrate after a nuclear attack . . . and how those who died first would be the lucky ones.

In its wake would be chaos, illness, and suffering that was virtually indescribable, and violent street gangs taking over everything that was not heavily guarded.

"So what's it all mean?" Betsy said.

"I don't know."

Betsy took the pages from me and skimmed them.

"Why would Sara want to know about nuclear installations and telekinesis? I don't see what one has to do with the other, do you? And did you notice there's an address scribbled here?"

"Yes, I saw the address, and I don't know, well, not exactly; not yet anyway. I want to think about it some more. In the meantime, we better go try and find a couple of old nags that won't throw us off and break our necks."

Betsy made a cute little face.

"I've got to tell you, Duvall, I'm kind of scared of horses."

I smiled. "So am I."

PART THREE

1

I didn't see how my horse could complain much about me. I let him pretty much do what he wanted.

If it was his desire to take me running through some bramble, we went through some bramble. Same for running fast. When he wanted to, we did, nearly getting lost a couple of times because we were so far ahead of the others. Likewise, slowing down. At one point, mid-afternoon or so, Henry, as he was called, just seemed to crap out. We lagged a good quarter of a mile behind the others.

Betsy's horse, on the other hand, must have gone to obedience school. Even the slightest tug on the reins got him to do exactly what she wanted. She tried not to look superior as we cantered along the floor of the valley.

If nothing else, my headstrong horse kept my mind off Emily. If she was sold to the Federation, we'd never see her again. I couldn't say I gave much of a damn about Sara. It's one thing to love humanity collectively. It's quite another to love each and every one of the little buggers individually.

The day was gorgeous and so was the scenery, the deep green of the Midwest with piney hills boxing us in on both sides, and the occasional rushing stream with fish literally jerking up out of the water. We saw dogs, cows, sheep, and deer. Above us, hawks soared and swooped on the warm air currents.

All I knew was that we were headed to Alison's compound where Mae planned to do a little wheeling and dealing. Seems Alison didn't have much of a food supply, not something to run short of when you've got two thousand men and women and children to feed day in and day out. Alison had learned everything there was to know about raiding, but almost nothing about agriculture. Mae was prepared to wheel and deal.

I spent a good part of the afternoon, especially when Henry dropped all the way back, thinking about the articles that had belonged to Sara.

I was working up a hypothesis, something that's always dangerous when you base it on so little information. But it seemed to me that the connection between the nuclear missile sites and telekinesis was unmistakable. Given Sara's almost psychotic belief in the justice of her cause, it was also scary as hell.

Mae gave no thought to catching up with the raiders. She dropped back to talk to us briefly. She said the raiders knew this terrain well, had faster horses, and had a head start. Anyway, she said, there was no particular reason to try and catch them. That would just force a confrontation and poor Emily might get killed in the crossfire.

After her visit, we rode on until the sky started streaking with the colors of dusk—that unlikely combination of blood red and golden yellow and deep mauve. The nightbirds started singing then.

Mae suggested that we settle down for the night, build a campfire, and get some sleep. She said we'd like sleeping under the stars.

"But what about snakes?" Betsy asked her.

"Oh, they won't hurt you," Mae grinned, "except for the poisonous ones."

Then she spurred her horse back up to the front of the eighteen-person posse.

Night on the prairie. The cowboys sitting around the campfire with their cups of coffee, a relaxing end to a hard day's ride. One of the cowpokes strums an old guitar and hums a Western ballad.

I used to watch the Western holos of Roy Rogers and Gene Autry and at least once per holo, you got that campfire scene.

Well, our campfire scene that night was a little different.

For one thing, the heat of the day had caused us to underestimate how cold it would be that night. Numbingly cold.

For another, the food we'd packed, mostly bread and food-substitute pills, looked pretty bleak sitting around the campfire. You could read the label that said FULL DAY'S VITAMINS AND MINERALS on the little packet Mae handed you. But that kind of reassurance wasn't what you wanted.

You wanted a roast beef sandwich. And some mashed potatoes with hot thick gravy. And some peas swimming in butter. And a piece of apple pie and a cup of coffee to top it off.

But what you got were three small pills in a packet.

Then there was the ground.

Now in every Western holo I've ever seen, cowpokes seemed to love sleeping on the ground.

Just pull that Stetson down over your eyes.

Kick your boots off.

Pull your blanket up.

And trundle off to dreamland.

Well, have you ever actually tried to lie down on God's hard green earth? Let alone *sleep* on it?

So what we did, all of us cowpokes and cow-pokettes, was sit around the campfire and bitch.

Maybe we weren't the greatest horse riders in the world, or the truest shots, or the ablest ropers, but the one thing we excelled at was bitching.

We bitched about the cold, the food, the ground, how the fire never quite got hot enough, how one guy's feet smelled something awful when he unshod himself, and how we were all probably going to be attacked by snakes or wolves or rabid bats and die right here in front of the campfire. These guys really *had* gotten used to living in the Settlement, just as I had gotten used to the relative luxury of life in a skimmer.

We got the bitching out of our systems, enough anyway, that Mae was able to start treating us like grown-ups again, and assigning two shifts of guards for the night, one guard, armed with a carbine, per shift.

And damned if one of the ersatz-cowboys didn't pull out a banjo which was, at first, a hell of a lot of fun to hear out here on the deep-shadow, full-moon, ass-freezing emptiness of the prairie.

After about sixteen songs, however, most of which sounded suspiciously alike, the sound of the banjo had begun to grate a mite. Apparently, I wasn't alone in my waning enthusiasm. Couple of the cowpokes made a big point of saying they needed sleep and thus some quiet.

The banjo guy looked real disappointed.

When everybody started settling in, Mae came over and sat down and we talked quietly.

"You really think this Alison will go for the swap?" Betsy asked.

Mae nodded, her face looking drawn and tired in the golden reflection of the campfire.

Mae hefted a saddlebag. It looked so heavy, she could barely lift it.

"Three bars of gold," she said. "And gold is still a very precious commodity out here. In fact, gold and antibiotics are the most precious things in the entire Zone."

"God, that's really great of you, Mae," Betsy said.

"I want to get the girl back for selfish reasons," Mae said.

"Oh?" I asked.

"I don't want the Federation to get their hands on her. The more telepaths they have, the stronger they'll be."

"I guess that makes sense," I said.

"Where'd you ever get three bars of gold?" Betsy said.

"There was a bank near the Settlement. We managed to get into the vault one day. We carried off about a million dollars in cash."

"Wow," Betsy said, "what'd you do with it?"

Mae laughed. "Had a nice big bonfire." She looked at our own pitiful little fire. "I wish we had it here tonight."

Mae yawned.

"Well, time for bed."

Mae winked at me. "Unless you want to get that banjo player to do a couple more numbers for us."

"No, thanks," I said.

"I didn't think so."

Mae walked over to the other side of the fire, took her blanket roll and bedded down for the night.

We went to work on our own blankets and were soon lying beneath the Western stars.

We held hands for a time.

Betsy said, "I counted up how many times I've thought about him in the last hour."

"The flyboy?"

"Uh-huh. Guess how many?"

"Twenty?" I said.

"Are you crazy? C'mon, be serious."

"Ten."

"No way."

"Eight."

"Lower."

"Five."

"One," she said.

"Wow," I said. "That makes me feel better."

"Well, I must be falling in love with you, Duvall, or else I'd be thinking about him all the time the way I used to."

"I guess that makes sense."

"Sure it makes sense. I'm finally falling in love with a nice, sensible guy."

I'm not sure that was anything I wanted to hear.

I mean, it's one thing to understand in an abstract sort of way that I'm this kind of ordinary, unremarkable guy. But it's another to have it confirmed by the woman you love calling you a "nice, sensible guy."

That sounds like a pair of shoes that are good for your feet, but you're embarrassed to wear out of the house.

"A nice, sensible guy," I said.

"Sure. There's nothing wrong with that."

"Sounds like you're settling for second best."

I tried to keep the hurt and self-pity out of my voice but it was difficult.

"You're not second best, Duvall. You're what I need."

"Like medicine that tastes bad."

"Don't go all sensitive on me, Duvall."

"Yeah, I guess I'm being sort of a baby, aren't I?"

"Anyway, we shouldn't be talking about ourselves. We should be thinking about Emily."

"I agree."

"So let's just lie here and think about Emily."

I thought about Emily for about thirty-two seconds and then I started thinking about myself again. And how much I loved Betsy and how much I was in pain *because* I was in love with Betsy.

When I finally got to sleep, I had this hollow feeling in my stomach. It wasn't going to work out with Betsy; it wasn't going to work out at all.

2

I slept so well that I didn't wake up until the first gunshot was fired.

I'd missed the three raiders sneaking up on our lone guard, missed the three raiders tying him up and gagging him, missed the three raiders coming into camp and shining their flashlights on every one of us, including me.

One of our guys made the mistake of trying to sneak his gun out from his blanket roll so he could get a shot at the raiders.

But they were too fast for him.

They put several bullets into his face and chest.

I woke up just in time to see the man, burnished in the campfire light, jerking about as the bullets entered his prone body. The sight wasn't one I'd forget for a while.

I started to my feet, but then I heard a gun cocked behind me.

"Stay right where you are," a woman's voice said.

I stopped moving.

By this time, Betsy was also awake. She sat up, looking confused but not especially afraid.

"Who's the boss here?" the one with the black hat said. She wore a denim shirt and denim pants. There were numbers stenciled across her back. Same with the other two women. Denims and numbers across the back.

"Who are you?" Mae said, getting to her feet.

"You the boss?" black hat said.

"Pretty much," Mae said.

"You tell them to cooperate or we'll kill them."

Mae stared at the women a long time. They were about the same age and body type. The other two were younger, taller, thin. They wore white Stetsons. They were trying to look tough. They were succeeding.

Mae glanced around the campfire. By now, everybody was sitting up, watching.

"Everybody cooperate," Mae said. "They already killed Bernie. It's pretty clear they won't hesitate to kill us, either."

"I want everybody to stand up, and empty his pockets," the black hat said.

The posse looked pretty tame right at this moment: sleepy, scared, docile. Maybe the Settlement didn't represent the pinnacle of civilization, but it was a hell of a lot more civilized than standing around a campfire in your stocking feet while three female desperadoes held guns on you.

One of the white-hatted ones had a big cotton

sack and she went around the entire campfire taking everything we pulled out of our pockets. She didn't pause to see if what she was getting was valuable. She told us to just dump it in the sack. When she got done, she walked over to the black-hatted boss.

"Now it's your turn," the black hat said to Mae.

"I already gave her everything I had in my pockets."

The woman laughed.

"Got a surprise for you," the black hat said. "We paid a little visit to your settlement. Pushed a couple of the guys around until they told us about the gold bullion you're bringing Alison."

The three women laughed again.

The black hat walked over to Mae and struck her with the butt of the rifle.

Blood erupted from Mae's mouth.

I started toward the intruder but Betsy put a hand on my arm. She was right. The black hat would bust my mouth for me, too.

"Where is it?" the black hat said.

"I don't know what you're talking about," Mae managed to say around the pain and the blood.

The second blow was even harder than the first.

This time, Mae almost went over backward.

I started across to the black hat, but then one of

the white hats turned and put her pistol right in my face.

"I'd love to kill you, asshole," she said. "I'd keep that in mind next time you're feeling brave."

I stepped back next to Betsy, ashamed that there was nothing I could do to help Mae.

"Now I'm going to ask you one more time," the black hat said to Mae.

Mae had her mouth covered with her hand. Blood seeped through her fingers.

"Tell her, Mae," I said.

The others spoke up, too, agreeing with me.

"Don't let her hit you again," one of the men said. "Just tell her, Mae."

Mae was stubborn and Mae was proud and she just might get killed for being both of those things.

My hunch was she was going to refuse the black hat at least one more time.

I didn't want to watch.

But the bloody mouth must have gotten to her and suddenly all the defiance went out of Mae's face and eyes.

She said, "I'll show you."

"No funny business," the black hat said.

Mae nodded and walked over to her blanket.

The saddlebags sat in the grass behind the bedroll.

The black hat followed her all the way over to the shadows outside the flickering light of the campfire, and kept her gun trained on Mae the whole time.

But Mae was a woman full of surprises.

As she bent over to pick up the saddlebags, I saw her start to twist around quickly.

The black hat didn't even get a chance to shoot straight.

Mae obviously knew she couldn't lift the heavy bags high enough to smack the woman in the face, so she settled for angling the saddlebags into the black hat's gun hand.

Three quick shots went wild, and then Mae dropped the saddlebags and sprang for the black hat, throwing a pretty good right hook into the other woman's face.

Just as Mae bent down to pick up the woman's fallen gun, one of the white hats opened fire, barely missing Mae's shoulder.

Everything stopped.

"Stand over there," one of the white hats said to Mae.

Mae didn't look very happy about it, but she didn't have much choice.

She reluctantly moved over a few steps, keeping her hands in plain sight.

The black hat picked up her gun and then walked over to Mae.

The slap came out of nowhere.

Mae was rocked backward. I saw her eyes close. The black hat had really hurt her.

"That's for being stupid," the black hat said.

Then she slapped her again, if anything, even harder.

"That's for knocking the gun out of my hand."

This time, the black hat didn't settle for a slap.

She went for a full punch.

Mae was staggered. I thought she might drop to her knees.

"That was for slugging me," the black hat said.

Then, as if she couldn't stop herself, the black hat got off a single hard straight jab to Mae's stomach.

This time, Mae did sink to her knees.

Silence once again around the campfire.

With one man dead, and Mae slapped around pretty hard, and the gold we were to trade for a young girl's life about to be stolen ... there wasn't much to say.

The black hat went over and picked up the saddlebags.

Where Mae had always grimaced when lifting the bags, the black hat seemed to have no trouble.

She simply hefted them and walked back to her horse.

The two white hats kept their guns on us.

Only when the black hat swung up on her horse did the other two follow.

When all three were mounted, the black hat looked at us and said, "Been nice doing business with you, folks."

Before they rode away, they stopped by the grove of pine trees where we'd ground-tied our horses.

There were four quick shots.

They chased our horses away.

3

One of the men had been a medic, so while the rest of us built up the fire and tried to put together some kind of breakfast, the medic worked on Mae's mouth.

He got the bleeding stopped, and after half an hour or so, according to Mae, the pain lessened.

As night turned into streaks of pink and red and gold, we hunched around the campfire trying to figure out what we were going to do.

Jack Myles, Mae's right-hand man, a big fierce guy with an Old Testament beard said, "There's enough traffic in and out of Alison's compound that one or two of us might be able to sneak in."

"But how do we know where they're keeping the girl?" I said.

"From what I remember of the compound," Myles said, "there're probably only a couple of places where she could be. I can draw a map of the inside of the compound for you."

Mae, still talking around her painful mouth, said, "Jack used to be one of Alison's men."

"What happened?" I said to Myles.

He shrugged.

"I was on a raid where they killed some children. I finally saw them for what they were. Plus, I always felt bad about selling drugs to Federation agents, turning all those kids into addicts."

"How far are we from the compound?"

"A day, maybe a day and a half," Myles said.

I looked around the campfire.

"Are all you men still with us?" I said.

Only one man shook his head.

"I've got a bum left leg," he said, looking guilty.

"He can barely walk on it," Myles said. "He'll have to turn back."

"The rest of you?" I said.

They all nodded.

We spent the next half hour packing up the remains of the campsite. There wasn't much. Food tonight was probably going to be nuts and berries. Survival food, as it used to be called.

By the time daylight filled the valley with golden rays of sunlight, we'd set out on the day's journey.

"I sure hope we can find her," Betsy said, as she fell into step next to me.

"I sure do, too," I said.

4

For the first hour or so, I had a good feeling about a day-and-a-half walk.

I felt as if I were walking through history.

The fiery hills and rushing creeks and animal cries put me in mind of the Indian days, when the first white men walked this land. Except for electrical poles, we saw very little evidence of civilization. I could hear phantom tom-toms and war whoops and war chants. It was a pretty good feeling for an overgrown boy like myself.

I guess it was the second hour when I realized that my right foot was beginning to rub against the contours of my shoes. I was working on a blister, and a painful one. It was rapidly becoming far harder to ignore than the bruises I'd gotten when those two goons worked me over the other night.

Then the prospect of a day-and-a-half trek didn't sound so good at all.

I stopped every twenty minutes or so to beat, bend, and bang my right boot into submission.

But it wouldn't submit. No matter what I did to it, the damned thing kept gnawing at my foot.

I decided to walk with one shoe on, one shoe off.

This went all right until I stepped on a piece of glass and cut myself pretty good. So much for being far away from civilization. The culprit was a smashed Pepsi bottle from long ago. Something the Indians probably didn't have to worry about.

Betsy cleaned it out for me in a creek, and got it bandaged with a section of cloth from my undershirt, and then we went back to walking.

Early in the afternoon, we heard the calls for help. We weren't sure what they were, but at least one of the voices belonged to a small girl.

The truck was an old flatbed, and on its back rested a cage made of steel bars. A large padlock kept everybody locked inside.

In this case, everybody turned out to be a mother and two small children.

I used Mae's field glasses for a closer look.

They weren't easy to look at, the mother and her two small children. I suppose they most resembled apes, so flat were their faces, so hairy their bodies, and yet there was also something feral in the eyes and elongated mouths. They made shrill, keening noises that I'd never heard before, plaintive, haunting.

The truck had a flat tire. Two Normals jacked up the left front side of the truck and were working on the tire. One reason that so few

Zoners used cars and trucks was because gasoline was hard to come by, and tires were so unreliable. That's why horses were the preferred method of transportation.

Three more armed men leaned against a nearby tree, watching the tire-changing.

"Bounty hunters," Mae said.

"I don't understand," Betsy said.

"There's a Federation holo show called *Monsters and Mayhem*, " Mae said. "If you find a mutation freaky enough, you take it to Alison and she'll pay you for it. Then she'll turn around and sell it to her Federation friends for about twenty times as much money."

"God," Betsy said, "it's bad enough that she sells drugs, let alone people."

Mae nodded.

"They put these poor people on the holo maybe seven or eight times in a holo season, and then kill them to make room for new creatures. Alison probably sells them a couple of hundred people a year."

She took the field glasses from me for another look.

"That's Mason and Proffit. They're the most notorious bounty hunters in the Zone."

The caged creatures kept squealing.

It was hard to listen to.

Bad enough that they'd been born that way. Now they were prisoners, as well.

"I'd like to go down there and free them," Betsy said.

"So would I," Mae said. "But we'd probably get a couple of our own killed in the process."

She looked at me.

"You agree, Duvall?"

"Yeah, I do. We can't afford to lose anybody else, or use up our firepower, Betsy."

"But those poor creatures—"

"It's them or Emily," I said gently.

Mae said, "Sorry. That's the way it's got to be."

Just then, the mother managed to break a rusted bar off and, shoving her kids out of the cage, she screamed to them to run away and run fast.

They did.

One of the armed men came out and picked up a rapierlike length of metal and stabbed the mother with it.

You could hear the buzz all the way up where we were.

The mother's hair literally stood straight up as she received the voltage from the prod.

It wasn't easy to watch.

It wasn't easy to just let pass.

"C'mon, you two," Mae said, sensibly enough. "We'd better get going."

5

I counted at least fifteen farms that had been abandoned. Some of them still had tractors in the field. When the two men broke into the lab and loosed the virus on the United States, there hadn't been time for anything but fleeing or dying. And the trouble with fleeing was, there was no place to go.

And now, as Mae explained, it was too dangerous to live on a farm with just your family. To survive, the Normals out here had learned how to turn housing developments and small towns into bastions that dissuaded Alison and other raiders from attacking. It was interesting to me that most of the raiders were Normals. The mutants, at least those who were badly mutated, stayed in the shadows, just wanting to be left alone. I didn't blame them.

I walked alongside Mae for a few hours. We tried to figure out how we were going to get into the compound. From the way Mae described it, we sure weren't going to shoot our way in. We would be badly outnumbered.

We talked about going over the compound fence.

We talked about trying to slip in through a knot of compound people.

We talked about tunneling into the place.

None of these ideas appealed to either of us, but it was likely we'd have to adopt one of them if we wanted to see Emily again.

"You really think we can get in there?" Betsy asked me when I dropped back to walk with her.

"One way or another, we're going to get in there."

Betsy took in deep breaths. Butterflies put on shows for us, birds sang songs for us, grass grew just to impress us.

It really was too bad Emily wasn't here to enjoy it.

"I feel guilty enjoying this weather the way I am. I wish Emily could enjoy it." Then: "You'd be proud of me, Duvall."

"Oh, yeah?"

"Yeah. I went four hours without thinking about you-know-who."

"Congratulations."

"But that isn't even the big news."

"What's the big news?"

"You. I thought of you at least six times during those four hours."

She slid her arm through mine.

"I'm really going to do it right this time."

"Do what right?"

"You know, find the right kind of man for myself. And you're the right kind of man for me."

She squeezed my arm.

We walked on.

"Bad boys," Betsy said.

"Huh?"

"Do you ever watch *My Problem Is Your Problem?*"

"Is that the one where people come on and tell their secrets?"

"Yeah."

"I only watched it once."

"I can tell you didn't like it. You should've given it a chance."

"Maybe next time."

"They always have these women on who're attracted to bad boys. That's my hang-up, too. Bad boys."

"Ah."

"I can tell you really don't want to talk about this."

I was about to say something sarcastic when one of the men at the head of the line shouted "Halt!" and we all stopped.

I ran up front to see what was going on.

Mae had her field glasses trained on the piney hills in front of us.

She said she'd seen somebody moving quickly through the trees up there.

"Probably a scout for Alison," she said.

"Probably figuring out the best way for her to attack us. You want to look?"

She handed me the glasses.

At first, I didn't see anything, just the lengthening late afternoon shadows between the trees.

Then—there!

Between a couple of trees.

A person moving fast.

I didn't get a good look at all.

Just a human body shape.

"Any guesses?" Mae inquired.

"Probably a scout, just the way you said."

"You think we should keep going?"

"I wouldn't stop just because of one scout."

Mae nodded, gave the signal for everybody to start moving again.

"We'll be getting to the compound around nine or ten tonight, the way I figure anyway."

"I keep thinking about your idea of tunneling," I said.

"So do I."

"I suppose it could be done."

"You think you could do it?" she said.

"I'd sure be willing to try."

She smiled.

"I'll remind you that you said that."

At dusk, we stopped at a creek to wash up a little and have some food, such as it was, anyway.

I sat next to Betsy against a pin oak.

"You think she'd let us take her?"

"Emily?"

"Uh-huh."

"Probably not."

"We could give her a lot better home."

"I know," I said. "But that wouldn't make any difference to somebody like Sara."

"I suppose you're right."

The shout was as loud as a shot. I was on my feet in moments. I half-expected a raid. I hadn't been able to forget about that scout in the hills a few hours earlier.

Betsy was beside me. She'd scrounged an ancient Walther from one of Mae's men. Earlier in the day, she'd shown me how well she could use a firearm. She was damned good.

There was very little daylight left, so little that when Mae's men brought their prisoner back, I wasn't sure who it was.

There was quite a wrangle. Big as the two men were, they had to use a lot of skill and force to drag the prisoner into camp and over to Mae.

The prisoner was finally freed and pushed in Mae's direction.

"Tell them to take their damned hands off me," Sara Ford said, angry as usual. "And tell them to keep them off, too."

6

Within ten minutes, we were marching toward the compound again.

Sara Ford walked next to Betsy and me at the back.

"Is Emily all right?" Betsy said.

"For right now, she is. But if the damned Federation ever gets their hands on her—"

Whatever her other shortcomings might be, Sara was resourceful. She'd managed to overpower one of her guards and force him to escort her out through the front gate. Then she headed back toward the Settlement, hoping Mae would help her get Emily.

It had been Sara we'd seen in the hills this afternoon. Without field glasses, she couldn't be sure who we were or what we wanted.

When it got dark, she sneaked down to our resting place for a better look at us.

Now we walked along an old trail, the moonlight touching everything with silver and shadow. The night was sweet with the smell of spring and soft breezes.

"You left some papers behind," I said after a time.

Sara looked at me defiantly.

"You found them, huh?"

"Yeah."

"I want them back. Now."

"You can have them if you want. But I think I already know what you're up to."

"You can't prove a thing, Duvall, and you know it. In fact, I don't even give a damn if you give them back. I don't need them anymore."

And with that, she stalked up to the front of the line to talk to Mae.

"She's really mad."

"She's also bluffing," I said.

"About what?"

"About not caring that I know what she's up to."

"What *is* she up to?"

I told her.

"God, are you serious?"

"Uh-huh."

"But when they tried those experiments before—"

"—most of the people being experimented on died."

"Exactly."

"You don't think she could do that to Emily, do you?"

I laughed bitterly.

"Are you kidding? She's a revolutionary, Sara is. And to be a revolutionary means you're willing to sacrifice anybody for the greater good."

"Even your own child?"

"Even your own child."

We walked on.

The compound had once been a baseball stadium. The insides had been torn out to build a shelter for fifteen hundred people and to provide facilities for medical needs, blacksmithing, and food distribution. There were two entrances, front and rear, both heavily guarded. Alison's quarters were high up in the press box, which she'd expanded to turn into a military headquarters as well as a lavish apartment. Apparently, she took an endless succession of lovers, many of whom, when she was done with them, got pushed to their deaths from her aerie. Alison must have read up on the black widow spider.

We got all this from Sara, who dropped back to talk to us again.

"We've been thinking about tunneling our way in," I said.

"It's a possibility," she said. "Worth a try, anyway. The problem is, they took Emily yesterday afternoon, and I've got a terrible feeling that she's up in Alison's headquarters."

If that was true, then we'd have two break-ins to worry about—getting into the compound itself, then getting all the way up to Alison's aerie.

Sara was about to tell us more when Mae

stopped the ragged troops and held up her hand for silence.

"The compound is over that next hill. We'll have to be very quiet from now on."

We started marching again.

The hill was still muddy from a recent rain. When we reached the top, we looked down and saw a large bowl-shaped arena that was lit by dozens and dozens of torches and lanterns. The setup was like a huge outdoor bazaar contained within the walls of the stadium.

We stood behind a windbreak of pine trees.

Despite the time, early evening, hundreds of people moved around inside.

To the east, perhaps a quarter of a mile away, was a gigantic corral where perhaps five hundred horses were quartered.

To the west was a sprawling tent city.

Through Mae's field glasses, I could see that this was where at least a part of the army stayed. Even from here you could hear the drunken laughter of the soldiers. All of them were dressed in the black jumpsuits I'd seen the other day.

Mae and I started to look for a possible tunnel entrance. Was there any point in the exterior wall shadowy and unguarded enough to allow me to dig?

None of the possibilities looked great, but there was one, just where the wall started to curve on the west side, where there was a long, dark stretch that held no guard. Nor were there any guards walking point. The only armed soldiers we could see at the stadium were stationed at the entrances.

Mae handed me a collapsible military shovel.

"You think you can do it with this?" she said.

"If he can't, I can," Sara Ford said.

"You're not going," I said.

"The hell I'm not."

"Emily's her daughter," Mae said softly.

"She's right," Betsy said.

"I don't like you any better than you like me, Duvall," Sara Ford said. "But right now that doesn't matter. Getting Emily back is all I care about."

Right, I thought.

So you can destroy her yourself as soon as you get her where you want her.

"You'd better get going," Mae said.

I sighed. Sara was going to be with me whether I wanted her or not.

I took the shovel from Mae, checked my stunner, and was about to start off down the hill . . . when a familiar whine filled the night sky . . . and we saw turbo-rockets laying streaks of reddish flame across the stars.

A rather large ship was landing in the field behind the rear entrance of the compound.

There was only one group on the planet that could afford a ship this big and expensive and fast.

Even though it bore no insignia, the ship had to belong to the Federation.

I stood there and watched. This was too cynical even for a cynical bastard like myself.

Mae's story was true.

At least one element of the Federation regularly landed ships at the compound.

And if that part was true, so, probably, was the second part: some element in the Federation swapped merchandise for drugs, and then sold the drugs back in Federation-held lands.

For just a moment there I felt the way Sara did: the Federation had to be the most corrupt political force on the planet.

Bad enough that they encouraged teenagers to lynch Undesirables, they also enslaved the same teenagers with dreamdust.

7

I had my stunner in my hand as Sara Ford and I went down the dark hill.

The compound had come alive. In addition to delivering guns, the ship also served as a social event. It had brought its own power source. Huge floodlights blasted the area around the ship and rear entrance.

People of all ages crowded around the rear entrance to watch men in blue Federation jumpsuits off-load the massive ship. The ship's crew were celebrities to the compound people.

We circled wide so that we would skirt the edge of the crowd as we looked for the deepest shadows along the fence. Mae had given us loose-fitting rust-colored jumpsuits that a lot of people in the Zone wore. Even some of the compound crowd wore them.

At one point, an armed guard stepped out of the shadows to take a closer look at us, but just as he called for us to stop, there was some kind of commotion in the crowd, and he had to run over and see what was going on.

We hurried off, down the sweeping curve of the fence.

By now, the air of festivity had increased. Accordion music filled the air; so did the scent of alcohol. We saw a very drunk lady stagger over to a guard and impose a glass of some beverage on him.

He didn't look as if he wanted to take it.

The lady changed his mind by drawing his face down to hers and giving him a very seductive kiss.

He decided he wanted that beverage after all.

We spent the next five minutes looking for the appropriate place to start digging.

The grass was dew-covered.

The earth was a lot harder than we'd anticipated.

The collapsible shovel felt like a toy in my hand.

This kind of dirt would take all night to dig up with a tiny shovel like this one.

We had to find some more yielding earth.

Sara Ford was efficient, I had to give her that. She worked a few yards ahead of me at all times, looking for some ground that would be sandier or still muddy from the recent rain.

As yet, she'd found nothing.

I was just about to test out my shovel again when I saw the black-suited guard with the torch come upon Sara.

The way he was weaving, I could tell that his celebration had begun much earlier in the evening.

"Hey," he said, "it's you. Everybody figured you'd be long gone by now."

"And leave such charming company?" Sara said.

I was outside the flickering light of his torch.

I wondered how she was going to handle this.

"I've got to take you back to the compound," the guard said. He had a six-shooter in his right hand. The torch was in the left.

"You want to have a little fun first?" Sara asked.

"Fun?"

Apparently, the woman who'd seduced the other guard into drinking some liquor had inspired Sara.

She slid her arms around the guard's waist and then pulled him tight against her.

"You're a big one."

"In more ways than one," he responded.

He leaned down and stuck the sharp end of his torch into the dewy grass.

Moments later, his gun still in his hand, he was taking advantage of the gift Sara Ford had just given him.

She knew just was she was doing.

Very slowly, she turned the guard around so that his back was to me.

Her left hand waggled me forward.

I had to move quickly.

I decided that even if my collapsible shovel wasn't very handy as an earth-mover, at least it had other uses.

I got up behind the guard, who by now was moaning and muttering his lust, and applied the back of the shovel to the back of his head.

He went down immediately.

We dragged him back into the shadows along the fence. We got his black jumpsuit off and put it on me. Arms and legs were too long, but the way Sara had them rolled up, they would do the job.

"The shovel isn't going to work," she said.

"I know."

"This uniform isn't as good as an elite guard's outfit, but you could be one of the compound people loading the dreamdust onto the ship."

"That's a damned good idea."

She glanced at me angrily.

"What the hell did you expect? I have a lot of damned good ideas."

And you're modest on top of it, I thought.

While I put on the guard's uniform, she kept watch. A couple of drunks wandered by and flirted with her. She said that she'd be happy to join them if her husband wasn't coming right back. They made some nasty comments about her husband and moved on.

When I was finished, I walked up to her and she ordered, "Give me your stunner."

"No way."

"They'll spot you right away with a weapon like that."

"I'll hide it."

She smirked.

"Where will you hide it?"

"Right here."

But there was no right here.

There were slit pockets on either side, but neither was big enough to hide a stunner.

"We're on the same side," she said.

"No, we're not."

She shook her lovely head.

"You mean, even after you see a Federation ship land and trade guns for drugs, you still don't think we're doing the right thing?"

"Killing innocent people isn't the right thing. Ever."

"Sometimes, Duvall, it's the only way."

For one of the few times since I'd met her, I heard weariness, even fatigue in her voice.

Being a revolutionary twenty-four hours a day was apparently hard work.

Hating people took a lot of your energy.

I handed her my stunner.

"This'll be right here, waiting for you," she said.

"I'll see you in a little while," I said.

She smiled.

"Hopefully, anyway."

Walking around to the front entrance took me ten minutes. The revelers were drunker than ever. People kept bumping into me. A few wanted to fight, but I just kept on moving, letting their slurs bounce off me like soft stones.

The front entrance was clogged up with carts bearing various kinds of produce and breads and clothing. Mae had explained that a lot of farms sold directly to Alison in return for protection from her army.

I looked back along the line.

Far back was the truck we'd seen earlier, the one that had had the flat tire.

I felt a fleeting pity for the mutants in the cage. But there wasn't any way I could help them.

I turned and started walking through the entrance when the big man grabbed me.

He wore the black jumpsuit of Alison's army. His face was crosshatched with scars, obviously the result of torture. Somebody had worked him over for a long, loving time.

"I need to see your stamp," he said.

"Huh?"

Just then, two other soldiers walked through the gate and turned the backs of their hands to him.

He raised a small silver cylinder. A green beam of light peered out like an alien eye. The beam made contact with the tops of their hands and showed a red X.

Then I started noticing a guard on the other side of the entrance using the same kind of silver cylinder.

Same thing there.

People in black jumpsuits would walk through, holding up the backs of their hands as they did so.

And the guard, after seeing the proper red X, would wave them on through.

Sara had found out a lot, but I guess she didn't know about the X.

You didn't get to just walk through the entrance, after all. You had to show your ID.

"Let's see your hand," the big guy said.

"It's probably pretty faded. I went swimming tonight in the river."

"It's waterproof."

"Yeah, but I swam for a real long time."

"Hey, jerk-off," he said, "we got a lot of people waiting behind you, in case you haven't noticed. Now let's see your X."

As he spoke, he was pulling his Colt .45 from his Western-style holster.

He'd spotted me for a fake.

There was only one thing I could do.

I started to raise my hand, so he could see it better. This was with my right hand.

With my left, I was bringing up a haymaker.

The shock of the blow radiated all the way up my arm. The guard had a jaw like an anvil.

He wasn't in pain, but I was. Still, I'd distracted him enough so I was able to snatch his gun.

Then I turned and ran. Nothing else I could do.

"Hey!" he shouted, and people started looking at me.

A couple of them even tried to grab me, but I kept pushing and shoving my way to an open area, like a broken-field runner who can suddenly see daylight.

A shrill whistle sounded above the drunken din.

This meant more guards. This meant that I would never be able to escape.

As soon as I reached the gate, I looked left and looked right.

Guards from both sides were already responding to the whistle.

One of them saw me and shouted, "Stop!"

There was only one direction I could run. Straight ahead.

A couple of the people bringing produce looked as if they might step out from their carts and trip me. But they didn't. I was able to run pretty much uninterrupted until—

The bullet skimmed briefly along the top of my shoulder, tearing the jumpsuit fabric.

I allowed myself the luxury of glancing over my other shoulder.

There were six of them and, boy, did they look pissed.

I knew they'd kill me any time now.

I could try to outrun them, but there were too many of them for that. I cursed myself for giving up my stunner—and I didn't dare fire the Colt, not unless I wanted to draw even more attention to myself.

I saw an unattended cart piled high with sweet corn and threw myself beneath it.

Down on my hands and knees, I began crawling from cart to cart until I was seven or eight carts back.

I found one that had an underside I could hold on to. Sweating, my breath coming in hot gasps, my mind considering what I'd do if the guards found me here, I clung to the underside of the cart . . . and listened as they started shouting.

"He's gone!"

"Well, he couldn't have gone far!"

"You two men go over on the other side of the carts! Make sure he isn't hiding there!"

"And ask the drivers if they've seen anybody!"

Footfalls, heavy, intense.

More shouts.

Drivers saying that no, they hadn't seen anybody; and no, they wouldn't lie to the guards. Not ever.

Footfalls, again, only inches away from the cart where I was hiding.

"He's gone."

"That's impossible."

"Then where the hell is he?"

"Maybe he doubled back and tried getting into the compound again. There's a lot of congestion up there tonight."

"There are two guards at both entrances. No way he snuck in."

They started moving again, their voices disappearing in the frenzy at the entrance.

And they weren't the only thing that started moving.

The cart I was hiding under was drawn by an ancient plow horse. The ground reeked with his leavings and gave the flies an early Christmas.

The cart began to creak forward, and it was then I realized that what I held on to was part of the axle assembly and that I wouldn't be holding on much longer. The assembly was very mobile and would either rip off my fingers or dump me on the ground.

I had to risk running again.

I dropped to the ground, peeked out to first left, then right. There was no sign of any guards.

I started crawling under wagons again.

The night smelled of axle grease and horse droppings. Earlier, I'd been hungry. No more.

I heard their strange mewling sounds a few wagons away. The sound made me picture them vividly. The mutants in the cage, huddled and terrified. The kids hadn't been able to abandon their mother when they'd heard her cries of pain. But it had been a waste. Now she was dead and they were captives again.

I stopped.

Behind me came more footsteps, tramping the dirt, rushing forward.

"You're sure somebody saw him!"

"Yessir! My wife said she saw him, sir!"

They rushed on, headed in the wrong direction to find me.

I waited until they walked back his way before I moved.

"I should beat the shit out of you, you moron."

"Please, sir. It was an honest mistake."

"Your wife should lay off the dreamdust."

"She doesn't use dreamdust, sir. She really doesn't. We sell it, but we don't use it."

"Asshole," said the disgusted guard.

Then they were gone into the night, and I started crawling toward the back of the line again.

I had just figured out how I was going to get into the compound.

8

8

They must have been pretty tired, the mutants, because they slept through the ten minutes it took me to get the lock open. Sweaty, desperate minutes, I might add. Twice, I thought I heard guards approaching and had to duck under the cart.

The cage smelled pretty bad. The mutants had to use the floor of the cage as their toilet.

They looked like brother and sister apes, the two of them as they sat up and looked at me. The brother had some kind of breathing problem. Whenever he exhaled, he sounded as if he were choking.

I held the cage door open for them and said, "Hurry!"

They glanced at each other, then back at me.

Who was I, anyway?

And was this some kind of nasty trick I was playing on them?

"Hurry!" I said again.

If they could speak, they didn't let me in on the secret.

The female one scrambled to her feet first, her apelike eyes considering me for a long moment as I said "Hurry!" again.

She walked over to me and said, "You're really going to set us free?"

Her elocution startled me. She sounded like a college professor.

"Yes," I said.

"Why?"

"It doesn't matter. All that matters is that you get out of here right now."

She looked back at her brother.

He'd thrown off the blankets and was standing up.

They both stood about four feet tall. They would have been perfect simians except for their noses: they had ridiculously aristocratic noses, like Roman senators. The noses didn't go with the rest of their features.

I peeked out around the cage.

At the far end, two armed guards were walking this way.

"How do we know this isn't a trick?" the brother said. "You let us get outside the cage and then you tell everybody we were trying to escape. So you kill us."

"I'm not going to kill you."

I checked on the guards again.

They were coming closer with every passing moment.

"Hurry," I said to the female. "This'll probably be the last chance you ever have to escape."

"He's right," she said to her brother.

"What if he's tricking us?"

"I'd rather die trying to escape than be a freak on one of their holo shows."

The brother sighed, glanced at me.

"I guess you're right there," he said.

He took his sister's hand, and they walked to the cage door.

I stood aside, so they could drop to the ground, which they did.

I thought of all the perils that lay before them. This kind of mutant would be sought by every bounty hunter and holo producer working the Zone.

These two would probably be captured again within a few weeks—unless they had some kind of equalizer.

Just then, the brother began making the strange, sick sound he'd been making when I saw him earlier. He sounded as if he were dying.

"His lungs," his sister said.

I handed her the Colt.

"What's this?" she asked.

"A weapon to even the odds. But don't use it unless you have no other choice, because once you're out of bullets, that's it."

Tears glistened in her eyes.

"Can you believe that, brother? Somebody who actually cares about us?"

She handed her brother the Colt and then put her arms out.

I slid into her embrace.

Her body hair was covered with flies and tics and mites, but at that moment, I didn't care.

She probably hadn't had much affection since she was a child, if then.

"Thank you," she said.

I checked on the guards.

They were six carts away. At most.

"Hurry," I said again.

They set off across the vast dark prairie.

I climbed up into the cage, put the lock back on so that it appeared to be engaged, and then quickly plumped up some old clothes the two had worn. I lay one of the two blankets over the plumped clothes. As long as the guards didn't check carefully, this would look like one of the mutants asleep under the blanket.

I put myself under the next blanket, curling myself up into a fetal position.

The only part of me exposed was the top of my head.

At least up there, I had as much hair as the mutants did.

I lay still, waiting to hear the guards.

They walked on past, apparently just checking things out in general.

I lost track of time as I lay there. I even dozed off briefly, I think.

Someone shouted, "Move that wagon of yours, mister!"

Two heavy men sat on the front seat of the wagon. The vehicle moved at last. It took four different moves to get us all the way up to the compound gate.

After that, things moved quickly

The cart was drawn inside the compound. I could smell the sweat, alcohol, and latrines.

I could hear the laughing voices.

And I could feel my nervous system get cranked up. I'd been one ingenious sonofabitch getting in here but—

How was I going to get out?

9

I allowed myself to open one eye and look around the inside of the compound. The wagon was moving slowly.

There were probably a hundred small huts and tents used for housing. Women, children, and men of all ages wandered around the center of the stadium drinking, arguing, bartering.

The ladder leading to the converted press box was near the back of the compound.

The wagon driver seemed to know just where he was going.

He traveled sluggishly for several long minutes, then turned a hard right and drove straight to the northeast section of the compound.

Four wagons were lined up for inspection.

The two drivers jumped down from the wagon and walked to the head of the line.

"We're going to get some brew for ourselves," the driver said.

"Y' aint' supposed to do that, mate," said the inspector.

"Aw, hell, ain't nothin' we can do just sittin' here," said the other wagon man.

The inspector sighed.

"All right," he said. "But get back here in fifteen minutes."

"Sure thing," the driver said.

I watched them walk away, get caught up in the crowd.

Sounds: music, laughter, curses, more laughter.

Sights: a couple of half-naked hookers trying to persuade a very old man to go with them. A little girl of maybe five standing in the center of the compound and shrieking for her mother, all the time rubbing the hot tears that filled her eyes. Inspection points that were lined up with wagons carrying everything imaginable—squash, dreamdust, sides of beef, live chickens, limestone, mutants, and vats marked MINERAL WATER. There were soldiers, compound guards, punks looking for fights, nervous old men trying to avoid any kind of trouble at all. There were virginal girls, beautiful girls, ugly girls, angry girls, hookerish girls. And there were dogs, cats, mice, and rats underfoot.

I waited until the inspector hopped up on one of the other wagons, then I made my move, slipping out from under the blanket and crawling quickly to the front of the cage.

"Look! That mutant is tryin' to get out!" a kid of eight or so shouted to his brother, who was probably all of forty-six inches away.

His shout attracted the stares of a few more kids.

MUTANTS ESCAPE!

That was the kind of melodramatic headline that would be playing in their heads.

Kids loved to be scared.

As I undid the lock, I made claws of my hands and made fangs of my teeth and growled at them.

By now, there were six of them and they stood right up next to the wagon, all freckles and pug noses and straw-thick hair.

But my act wasn't convincing.

"He ain't no mutant," one kid said.

"The hell he ain't," said another, "or he wouldn't be in that cage."

I didn't plan to be in the cage much longer.

Now that I had the lock undone, I slipped it free, then opened the cage door.

"Hey, mister!" one of the helpful little bastards shouted. "Your mutant's gettin' away!"

The inspector, who was now two carts away, turned around and saw me in the door of the cage.

Saw the cage door open.

Saw me about to spring to freedom.

He pulled a very mean-looking pistol of some kind and came running toward me, letting his clipboard and pencil hit the dust.

I jumped down from the wagon bed and right into a circle of the kids who'd been watching me.

"See, he ain't no mutant," one of them said.

"You are too a mutant, ain't ya?" said his argumentative friend.

But I didn't have time to settle their argument for them.

All I could do was take off running.

Just as I managed to work my way into the crowd massing in the center of the compound, I heard a whistle shrilling behind me.

I'd lost the inspector temporarily, but he had the advantage of the whistle.

Now everybody in the compound would be alerted to the fact that a mutant had escaped.

Acting relaxed was my best hope.

I forced myself to slow down, did a few silent yoga exercises to calm my mind, and began walking slowly around the center of the compound, looking at the bazaar and its various wares. I could only hope no one would notice the shape my jumpsuit was in.

The whistle went off two or three more times. A voice on a speaker system said: "All unregistered mutants are ordered to report to the police box immediately. All unregistered mutants."

Like most places, the compound was willing to let you live free if you had a certain skill they needed. For instance, nobody balked at a medical doctor who had eight fingers. Even with the extra digits, he or she was a very valuable commodity.

These were the registered mutants.

All the others, just like the Undesirables in the Federation, were subject to swift and unmerciful death if they were caught.

I took my time at various stops along bazaar tables. Most of the jewelry and trinkets were junk, stuff dug up from some long-abandoned discount store. Anything very valuable would have been hoarded.

The loudspeaker again made the announcement about unregistered mutants reporting. I was waiting for people to start staring at me. Guilty conscience, I suppose. But nobody stared.

I kept moving inexorably to the rear of the compound, near the back entrance where the Federation ship was now being loaded up with large sacks of refined dreamdust. There was probably a large factory somewhere in the vicinity of the compound. There would have to be to fill this many sacks.

"Nice, huh?"

The hooker couldn't have been much more than eighteen or so. She was cute in a shabby sort of way. Her makeup gave her a look that was both comic and a little bit sad. She was too young to be as hard as she seemed.

She pointed to a shiny piece of junk jewelry, a bracelet covered with a dozen tiny, shiny mirrors.

"Yeah," I said, "nice."

"Why don't you buy it for me?" she said.

She was a bleached blonde and wearing a blouse that was opened all the way down to her navel, exposing sumptuous young breasts. Which she rubbed against my arm. She smelled of perfume and sweat and taut flesh.

"I wish I had some money."

"You better have some money," she said, "or you're in big trouble."

Her words brought my head around. I stared at her for a time.

"My little brother saw you," she said.

"Your little brother?"

"Yeah, one of the kids who was standing outside the cage when you were in it."

"Oh."

"He says you're a mutant."

"He does, huh?"

"Yeah, and I say I don't give a shit *what* you are as long as you buy me that bracelet."

"Unfortunately, I wasn't kidding."

"No money?"

"No money."

"Then I'm going right over there and tell that guard who you really are."

"You think maybe he'll get you the bracelet?"

"Well, you won't."

I smiled.

"I said I didn't have any money. I didn't say I wouldn't get you the bracelet."

"How'll you get it without any money?"

"You ever heard of theft?"

Now she smiled.

"You really think you could grab it?"

I nodded.

"Just give me a few minutes here," I said.

I'd been planning my little routine ever since she asked for the bracelet. I walked down to the end of the long table where the junk jewelry was displayed, looked around to see that nobody was paying me any special attention and then proceeded to trip and fall into the table, knocking a good deal of trash merchandise to the ground.

The owner, predictably, got very angry. He didn't care if I'd had a stroke or not, he was worried about his merchandise. And he was worried about people stealing it from the ground.

He was a small black man with woeful eyes and a good working knowledge of some of the more arcane vulgarisms.

He raced down to my end of the table, pushed me aside, and dropped to his knees, picking up necklaces, earrings, bracelets, chokers and other examples of his soddy wares.

Most of the people who'd been shopping at his table simply moved over to the tables of other merchants. There was nobody here to haggle with, and haggling seemed an integral part of this entire process.

In the meantime, I filled my pocket with several items, and then took the girl by the elbow and led her through the crowd.

"You didn't get them, did you?" she said.

"Of course I got them."

"Really?"

"Really."

"Wow. You want to have sex?"

I looked at her and smiled.

"Now I'm an okay guy, right?"

"I really wanted that bracelet."

"How about you do me a favor?"

"I already said I'd have sex with you. Free."

"Not sex."

"You don't like me?"

I laughed.

"I do like you, actually, against my better judgment. But I'm in kind of a hurry."

"For what?"

I nodded to the converted press box high above the compound.

"I need to get up there."

"You're crazy. That's where Alison lives."

"I know."

"How come you want to get up there?"

"I don't have any time to explain. But I do need your help."

We walked around the compound for the next few minutes. She looked greedily at all the merchandise displayed on the various tables. I felt sorry for her. She seemed like a nice kid. This compound would be her whole life until they turned her out someday, after her youthful appeal was history.

I explained to her what I needed done. She seemed intrigued by the challenge.

"What if he doesn't like me?"

"If he doesn't like you, something's wrong with him," I said.

"Thanks for saying that. It makes me feel better."

"You ready?"

"Uh-huh."

"I probably won't see you again. So here you go—"

I reached in my pocket and brought out the other trinkets I'd stolen.

They filled both of her cupped hands.

She got tears in her eyes and I felt sorry for her all over again. So easily satisfied; such sad little expectations.

"I wish you'd have sex with me," she said.

I leaned over and gave her a fatherly kiss on the forehead. Unfortunately, as I was leaning, the back of my hand brushed against one of her full, firm breasts. My groin forgot all about fatherly kisses and started thinking about a different kind of kiss altogether.

She sensed my sudden erotic interest, and smiled.

"I'll bet we could have a real nice time together," she said.

I sure couldn't deny that.

I gave her a little push toward the ladder leading to the press booth.

"You'd better go."

All she needed to do was distract the elite guard long enough for me to pull him back into the shadows, knock him out, and take his uniform.

She worked her way through the crowd to the area beneath the press booth, and went to work.

At first, he didn't seem particularly vulnerable to her.

He simply nodded yes, no, yes to her first

questions. Then she said something that got him to smile. Then she said something else that caused him to move a few steps closer to her.

I felt a bit sleazy using her this way, but she was a working girl, and compared to some of the things she'd probably done, this was nothing more than a little harmless fun.

She slid her arm around his waist, and smiled up at him.

They exchanged more words in pantomime. I decided it was a good time to move.

Between the ladder and the rear wall of the compound was a shadowy area perfect to hide in.

I walked through the crowd, and when I got close to the ladder, I cut right sharply, hurrying into the shadowy area.

By this time, my young friend had completely captivated the black-suited soldier with the sort of Robin Hood silver hat the guards wore.

He was smiling and laughing and he couldn't keep his hands off her.

I waited in the shadows.

Another guard came along.

I had the terrible feeling that the first guard was about to be relieved.

My young friend would have to start all over.

But the second guard only lingered a minute or so, discussing something quickly with his compatriot. Then he was gone.

The girl nodded to the shadows behind the guard.

He looked around, left to right, right to left.

He'd probably been rendered deaf, dumb, and blind now by his lust. You know how you get.

A quick little turn in the shadows next to the wall. What was the harm? Who would see? You could manage it in such a way that nobody would even be sure what you were doing out there. One thing that lust leads to is creativity.

She lured him back, and he gladly followed.

As soon as they reached the shadowy area, she turned him around so that his back was to me, and began kissing him.

That was when I came up with the bottle I'd found and hit him twice across the back of the skull.

He was nice enough to collapse immediately.

I dragged him back into the shadows, swapped his elite, uniform for what I was wearing, bound and gagged him with strips torn from my jumpsuit, and then took his weapon.

A few minutes later, I emerged in his clean black uniform. Now I had a jaunty little silver hat on my head.

"I do all right?" my young friend said.

"You did fine."

"You want to have sex with me now?"

"Honey, I've got to go up to the press box. I'm sorry."

"I think you're crazy."

"Maybe I am."

She pouted momentarily

"Lots of men want to have sex with me."

"I know. I'm one of them."

"Really?"

"Really," I said, and it was true. But right now there was work to be done—and there were my feelings toward Betsy to consider. I was born the faithful type.

I said, "You wouldn't turn me in, would you?"

I had this fear that she'd be mad because we hadn't had sex, and would turn me over to a guard as soon as I started up the ladder.

"No way," she said. "You gave me the bracelet and the other stuff, remember?"

"Good girl," I said. "I appreciate it."

I looked up the long, long ladder.

"Well," I said. "Wish me luck."

I gave her another fatherly kiss, this time being careful not to nudge her lovely breasts, and then went over and started climbing.

10

Halfway up the ladder, the headache hit me.

It came on so strong, so sudden, that I was momentarily immobilized.

I was half-afraid that the headache would weaken me so much that I'd fall backward off the ladder. I gripped tight enough to cause pain.

It wasn't a general headache, or even an arcing one. It was concentrated with the intensity of a knife slash behind my left eye. After a few moments, it began to throb, pulsate, leaving me blind and weak.

I wondered if somebody below had fired some kind of new weapon at me. While I was way past the top of the wall, on maybe the twenty-fifth rung or so, I was still within range of most weapons.

A general feeling of dizziness; a sudden vortex of blindness; cold sweat; trembling.

The sensation that I was going to fall over backward—

I gripped the ladder tighter, tighter, and clung

on, hoping that this experience, whatever it was, would soon pass.

Slowly, I opened my right eye, looked below.

Seen from up here, the center of the compound resembled a carnival midway. Circles within circles of people walking around, trying out this table or that booth, a general air of festivity creating smiles and laughter. They looked small from up here, all the people, and they reminded me of how much I hated heights. Flying had never bothered me but ladders scared the hell out of me. Go figure.

Please help me, Duvall. Please.

I started climbing again.

Please help me, Duvall. I'm in Alison's office.

At first, I assumed it was some kind of guilt on my part. I felt bad about poor Emily being kidnapped, so she was in my mind, pleading for me to help her.

I kept climbing.

While the worst of the headache had subsided, the cold sweats and the voice in my mind remained.

I know you can hear me, Duvall. Talk back to me. Just use your mind.

I still wasn't ready to accept what was pretty obvious by now. Sure, Emily had as extraordinary gifts as a psi student's, but inhabiting somebody else's mind, and then urging that person to respond in kind—

I'm really here, Duvall.

I'm not imagining this?

No, you're not.

She then explained to me how the huge press box, which had been expanded to become both an office and an apartment, was laid out.

She told me what to expect when I knocked on the door, what to expect when I got inside.

The trick, she said, was to knock out the front door guard, and then the guard at the hallway leading to the back, and Alison's office.

They've already called somebody in the Federation who is going to pay a lot of money for me. They're taking me back on the Federation ship that they're loading up now. I'm scared, Duvall. If the Federation gets me, I'll never be able to see Betsy or you again.

Then she added: *I want to see my mother again, too.*

Somehow she didn't sound as happy about seeing her mother as she'd sounded about seeing Betsy. Or me, for that matter.

I was nearing the top of the ladder now.

You climbed all the way up to a door where you were admitted by the guard.

Do I need some kind of special pass to get in?

There's a code word, Duvall. Just a minute.

She read a door guard's mind, apparently.

The word is "Birthday." Tomorrow is Alison's birthday.

Thanks.

I took the remaining rungs quickly.

When I reached the last rung, I climbed up onto the platform that ran all the way around the press box.

I tried not to look down.

I really did have a thing about heights.

I looked at the guard on the other side of the glass door.

"Password."

"Birthday."

He nodded.

The door was buzzed open.

I went inside.

Halfway across the threshold, I seized his throat, squeezed it so hard that he went limp within seconds.

I helped him fall to the floor so he wouldn't make any noise, and then I bound and gagged him with more strips I'd saved from my old jumpsuit, and dragged him over to a nearby closet.

I searched him, but I didn't find anything useful.

I took a right and started walking down a long, narrow hallway where another black-garbed guard waited.

"Password," he said.

"Birthday."

He nodded.

This one wasn't so easy.

I stepped forward to grab his throat, but either I was too slow or he was too fast.

He came at me with the butt of his pistol.

I put a fist deep into his stomach, then brought my knee up to his groin. The pain distracted him momentarily. I was able to rip the gun from his hand and use it on him. I brought it down hard against the side of his head. He had the decency to slide into unconsciousness.

I hit him a second time. I wanted to be sure he stayed unconscious for a time. I emptied his pistol and pocketed the bullets.

The hallway floors were carpeted. Any sound we'd made had probably been absorbed pretty well. The lighting was indirect and came from the ceiling. Looked good, I suppose, but was too fancy by half. It left long shadows in the hallway.

Hurry. Alison heard you.

I reached down to the man's belt and found a small black box that looked as if it would open certain doors automatically.

I got my weapon ready just about the time two guards, apparently summoned by Alison, came running around the far corner of the corridor.

I put two bullets in each of them.

They didn't have time to squeeze off a single shot.

I pointed the black box at the electronic device on the door leading to Alison's office. The door slid open.

I went in with my gun ready, but Alison was waiting for me.

She was a trim, blonde woman of maybe forty years with a striking, if not beautiful, face. She wore the familiar black jumpsuit of her army without any extra decorations or doodads. Around her thin hips was slung, gunfighter-style, a holster that would ordinarily have held a high-powered stunner.

She wasn't as imposing as I thought she'd be, but then they probably never were, the historical figures we hold to be so fierce and godlike. Napoleon suffered from very bad gas attacks; Attila the Hun had bladder problems; and Abraham Lincoln was so manic depressive that he frequently fled the president's office to go weep in a small side room. Alison here probably had a bad case of dandruff. But even if she didn't, she was a creature of legend. Just a nice-looking, bright, and very ambitious woman who'd managed to put together a formidable army, and to make a deal with her ostensible enemies, the Federation.

Right now, that particular stunner happened to be in her left hand. The muzzle was pushed against Emily's head.

Emily sat in a chair in the middle of the large but mostly empty office. The wall was filled with different maps of the Zone. Alison's own holdings, or at least land which she dominated, comprised about a quarter of the entire Zone. The maps also indicated areas that she obviously planned to move into.

"You won't kill her," I said.

"You're sure of that, Mr. Duvall?" Alison said.

"She's too valuable."

"It may come down to my life or hers." She smiled. "By the way, set your gun down on the desk over there."

I didn't have much choice,.

"I've already made contact with some of my friends in the Federation," Alison said. "Emily will be going back with them tonight."

But I knew that already.

"Has she hurt you, Emily?" I said.

Emily, who had been crying, and who looked wan and scared, shook her head.

"Now if you'll excuse me, Mr. Duvall, I'll call two more guards. Seems you killed the last two."

I was listening to Alison but watching Emily. A tremor passed through her body, a spasm that shook her for perhaps as long as thirty seconds. I wondered if she was having some kind of epileptic seizure.

A noise caught in her throat; a faint but foreboding scream.

She sat up straight in the chair suddenly, straining against her ropes, and then turned her very pretty face toward Alison.

I wasn't sure what was happening at first—I mean, suddenly the stunner in Alison's hand began glowing—and then she dropped it quickly and grabbed at her gun hand, crying out in pain.

Then I saw the dropped stunner ignite a piece of paper on the desk.

Emily had used her powers to turn the stunner into a piece of molten metal.

I didn't waste any time.

I ran over to Emily and started untying her.

Alison came over and grabbed me, but I got

her by the shoulders and flung her backward into the wall.

She hit hard, banging her head, but not hard enough. She ran to her desk and was about to punch a warning button when I grabbed her wrist, got her in a hammerlock, and then took the rope she'd used on Emily, and tied her up with it.

I set her down in Emily's chair. By now, Emily had the gag out of her mouth. She gave it to me. I used it on Alison, who looked affronted that I'd put the same spittle-soaked rag in her mouth.

Emily said, "Guards are coming. One of them has a rifle."

I dragged Alison over to a closet and put her in there. She tried to scream, but the gag silenced her. She tried to kick, but the ropes made it a feeble kick at best.

I grabbed Emily.

We pressed flat against the wall.

We could hear the guards now, coming down the hall.

Emily took my hand and squeezed it. She was trembling.

There were three of them, and they burst through the door, heading right for the center of the room.

That was when I stepped up and said, "If you don't put down your guns, I'm going to kill you all right now."

They looked pretty formidable in their scowls and black jumpsuits, but they knew that I could

kill at least two of them by the time they were
able to get me. They might be brave enough, but
they weren't stupid.

"Put them down now," I said.

Alison's desk was getting to be quite a gun
repository.

Her own stunner still sat there and was now
joined by two pistols and a rifle. When they'd
back away, I tossed the weapons out of the room.

"C'mon, Emily," I said, and took her hand
again.

We started easing our way to the door.

Emily went out first.

I kept my gun trained on the three guards until
I reached the threshold of the door. I pushed the
button on the little black box even as I edged outside. The door slid shut. Once again I emptied the
weapons of their ammunition, reloading my own
gun, and pocketing the extras.

We worked our way carefully down the hall.

I kept hold of her hand. I also kept my weapon
ready.

We reached the end of the hallway. There was
the door leading to the exterior platform and the
ladder.

No guards were in sight.

"Do you think you'll be all right on the
ladder?" I said.

"If you just help me get started, I'll be fine."

I hadn't thought of the difficulties a blind
person would have using a ladder. But then,

Emily was hardly a typical blind person. Not with her telepathic abilities.

"We'd better hurry," I warned.

We went through the door and stood on the platform. I tried not to look down, but it was difficult. My eyes seemed inexorably pulled toward the compound below, the milling crowds, the festive atmosphere.

Up here there was wind, and a keen view of the sweeping midnight stars.

I helped Emily over to the square opening that joined the ladder to the platform.

I held her hand as she turned around and got ready for her descent.

Once, she started to trip and I grabbed her. Adrenaline rushed through me. I had an image of her falling to her death.

I shook my head, forcing the image from my mind.

She got turned around and started feeling about with her foot to find the first rung.

Once she made that connection, the rest was relatively easy.

She found the second rung, and then the third and fourth.

All this time, I'd been hanging on to her hand.

But now she said, "I'll be fine. You don't need to hold me anymore."

"You're sure?"

"Positive." Then: "Oh, God."

"What?"

"Guards coming."

"You sure?" I asked, even as I started following her down.

She was sure, all right.

Just then the door opened up and two hulking black-garbed guards stood glaring down at us.

11

"Go ahead!" I shouted to Emily.

"What's wrong?" she said, unable to see.

"Just start climbing down." I said.

The guards were already through the door. One of them had turned around and was starting down the ladder.

I wanted to move away from him quickly, but I couldn't because if Emily moved too fast, she'd make a mistake and fall off.

Emily moved at the best speed she could.

I made the mistake of glancing down again. The center of the compound looked dismayingly far away.

"Are you all right?" Emily called to me.

"I'm fine," I answered. "Just worry about yourself."

To speak to her, I'd turned around and put my head to my shoulder.

With my attention distracted, I hadn't seen what the guard above me was doing.

But I certainly felt it.

He'd moved down close enough to smash the heel of his boot into my fingers

He'd pinioned my hand to the rung of the ladder.

The scream I let out wasn't going to do my fantasy about being a he-man any good.

The guard weighed probably two hundred pounds and all of it seemed to be concentrated on my hand.

"Are you all right?" Emily cried out.

"Just go on! Get away!" I said.

Above me, I could hear the guard say, "I got the sonofabitch!" to his friend.

The pain was numbing.

I wriggled my hand left, I wriggled my hand right, but all my maneuvering did was bring more pain.

I had to stay calm enough to reason through this.

I looked at his foot, his ankle, the lower part of his leg.

I had one free hand.

Was there anything I could do to him with that one free hand?

I grabbed his ankle and tried to twist it.

But with all the weight on it, I didn't twist it very far.

The guard only ground down harder with his weight.

I grabbed the bunched muscle of his calf and tried to dig my fingers in deep.

He didn't budge.

There was only one thing to do, and again it wasn't anything you read about in the Hero's Manual.

I sank my teeth into his ankle.

He screamed.

But he didn't budge.

I bit harder. I could taste blood.

He screamed some more.

But he didn't budge.

If anything, he seemed to be pressing his weight even harder on my hand.

My pain was becoming intolerable, even though a good portion of my hand was numb by now.

And then he fell.

He made a big comic thing of it, the guard, like the star of an old two-reeler silent movie.

His hands lost their grip on the ladder. His arms started windmilling as he tried to reach the rungs again.

But Emily—and I had no doubt it was Emily doing this—wasn't about to let him hang on much longer.

He went over backward, coming down so close to me that I could smell his sweat and see his head as he passed me on the way down.

People below were already screaming and pointing at the big man falling down to the ground from almost the top of the ladder.

I watched him fall.

He fought all the way down, almost as if he were trying to do the breast stroke in some very deep water.

And he swore all the way down, too.

He landed in an area the crowd had cleared for him. In cartoons, bodies always bounce when they hit the earth.

But this guy didn't bounce.

He just lay there.

His body was just an outer casing now for dozens of broken bones and smashed organs.

Other guards came running over to him, weapons drawn.

Emily kept climbing down.

The three guards who'd come to check out their fallen comrade were now watching us.

We'd make it down the ladder, all right, but we'd walk right into their clutches.

Now I started climbing down in earnest.

About the time Emily had only a few rungs to go, the guards closed in.

That was when I saw Sara Ford.

She wore a black soldier's uniform now, too. She also had a stunner.

She walked right up to the three guards who were helping her daughter down from the ladder.

I couldn't hear what she was saying, but I watched it all in pantomime.

In a very discreet manner, so that onlookers probably didn't realize what was happening, she disarmed them.

Then she took Emily away.

"Hey!" I shouted down to her.

She looked up a moment, made eye contact,

and then hurried Emily through the crowd, toward the rear entrance.

She was leaving me to face the guards again. Just now they were picking up their weapons.

Then they raised their heads and told me to come down the rest of the way very slowly.

Sara had, predictably, double-crossed me. I'd found her daughter for her. Now she didn't need me any more.

I had a pretty good idea of where she wanted to go—Los Angeles, and the address on the papers I'd found.

I wondered how she was going to get there.

12

Even though the one guard had fallen to his death, the other guards were still waiting for me at the bottom of the ladder. With Sara gone, they'd recovered their weapons and were obviously eager to use them.

I didn't see much reason to stay in the middle of the ladder. Eventually they'd come up, or down, and get me; or they'd fire at me and I'd fall to my death.

I worked my way down the rest of the rungs. When I reached the ground, the three of them pointed their guns at me. One of them said, "Where did the woman go?"

I shook my head.

He slapped me, a hard openhanded slap that blinded me momentarily, and jarred my teeth.

"Now tell me, where did the woman go?"

We must have been putting on a pretty good show for the crowd because a number of them had forsaken the bazaar tables, and were watching us.

"I don't know," I managed to say, tasting some

blood in my mouth. "And no matter how many times you hit me, I still won't know."

Just as my sight was returning, and the pain was lessening along my jawline, I had a hallucination.

I looked into the crowd and saw McClure, the Federation agent who'd been trailing me for days, staring at me.

But that was impossible. Why would McClure be here in the zone? Hard to believe he was the kind of agent who'd deal in contraband like drugs. He didn't seem the type.

Two of the guards took me roughly by the arms and shoved me in the general direction of a small building marked POLICE. One of the guards then walked briskly away. Obviously, he didn't think I was dangerous enough to warrant two guards.

The crowd still watched us. I wished I looked fiercer. It would have made for a better show.

But my ears were still ringing from the slap, and a few faint stars still rolled before my eyes. It would probably be a while before I was back to normal.

"Any sign of the woman?" one of my guards said to the guard standing sentry in front of the police station.

"Not yet. We've got men everywhere looking for her."

"I don't see how the hell she could have gotten away," my guard said.

The sentry moved several steps to his left and

opened the door for us. From somewhere inside came a terrible scream. Somebody was being tortured.

"Ralph knows what he's doing," my guard said.

"Ralph?" I said.

He nodded.

"Ralph is the person in charge of convincing prisoners to tell the truth."

"Ah."

"He'll make sure *you* tell the truth, too."

The prisoner inside screamed again.

I tried hard not to imagine what good old Ralph, who probably loved his work, was doing to the poor bastard.

The guard shoved me toward the front door of the police station. I was about to walk through when I felt the guard behind me suddenly fall into me.

My first thought was that he'd tripped over something, and simply bumbled into me.

But when I turned around, I found him falling directly toward me. His eyes were closed and there was a thin ribbon of blood trickling down the side of his face.

I was just about to grab him under the arms and drag him inside when I hallucinated again.

There was McClure, the Federation agent.

"Let's get him over there by the side of the building," McClure said. "Then let's get the hell out of here."

"Is it all right if I ask you what the hell you're

doing here?" I said, as we toted the body to the side of the building

"There isn't time for that now," he said.

We sat the guard in a chair. McClure had the idea of fixing him up as if he were just sitting there, taking a little break. It was a damned good idea, actually. Nobody would bother him for a while. Unless they noticed the blood on the far side of his face.

"C'mon," McClure said.

Both of us wore the black uniforms of Alison's soldiers, so we moved with ease through the crowd, leery people making way for us.

Just as we reached about the midpoint in the bazaar, I saw the Federation ship explode into the atmosphere. You could feel the rumbling in the ground, and in your feet, and running up your legs. It was a powerful ship, as the fantail flame and the speeding silver body proved.

I watched it for a long second. It was beautiful against the night sky.

"That's one thing you have to give us, Duvall," McClure said.

"What's that?"

"We sure know how to build rockets."

"That you do."

He looked at me. There was a hint of whimsy in his dark eyes.

"She's aboard that, you know."

"Who's 'she'?"

"Who else? Your friend Sara Ford."

"How'd she get aboard?"

He patted the stunner in his uniform.

"Just put her gun to the captain's back and told him that if he didn't take her and her daughter along, she'd kill him on the spot. Your Sara is a very persuasive woman."

"She's not 'my' Sara."

He smiled icily.

"Oh, that's right. You're the man who won't take sides." The smile vanished. "Well, let me tell you something, pal. You're going to take sides this time or I'm going to kill you."

I knew he wasn't kidding.

"Sara Ford has figured out where there's a very old installation of nuclear warheads hidden in the ground. The Federation's never figured out a way to disarm them safely. Sara is going to have her daughter move the warheads so that they're pointed directly at Los Angeles. She can do that telepathically. She's the most gifted psi the Federation has ever known."

So I'd been right. From the articles I'd read, I'd figured out that Sara Ford was going to try some kind of nuclear blackmail. With the help of her daughter.

"There's just one problem for Sara," he said.

"What kind of problem?"

"Our experiments with psis have taught us that some kind of ESP tasks are so big, they destroy the psi forever."

"Meaning what exactly?"

"Meaning that Emily Ford won't have any trouble redirecting the warheads at Los Angeles.

And she won't have any trouble firing them. But the whole thing will probably render her insane the rest of her life. We've got a couple of them like that in a mental hospital right now."

"And Sara Ford—"

"Sara Ford being Sara Ford," he said, "won't give a damn at all. She'll just see Emily's breakdown as the price she has to pay for being a part of the grand and glorious revolution."

We walked a few more feet and he said, "I've got a small skimmer in the woods not too far from here. I've been trying to find you for the last twenty-four hours. We've still got time to stop Sara if we hurry—and if we're lucky."

All I could think of was Emily being insane the rest of her life. And in a mental hospital.

"How'd you know I was here?"

"Your friend," he said.

"Betsy?"

"Uh-huh."

"You know where she is?"

He smiled again.

"I know exactly where she is. In my skimmer waiting for you."

He started walking faster.

"We've got to haul ass, Duvall," he said. "You want to save Emily. And I want to save Los Angeles."

As soon as we got outside the compound gates, we started running.

PART FOUR

1

The tarmac was alive with the sound of gunfire.

One thing you have to give LAX—it's more exciting than most VR games. It's estimated that more than one hundred Undesirables a day touch down at LAX, and probably half of them are shot or chewed to ribbons right on the tarmac by the most relentless guards and guard dogs you'll find anywhere.

Of course, guards and dogs occasionally make mistakes and kill innocents, and when that happens you just haul your butt to the sixth floor of the airport and file a complaint with the Apologies Department. You receive, among other things, a large cash settlement, a sincere letter of remorse from the President of the Federation, and a license that gives you twenty-four hours to find the offending guard and kill him legally. If you kill him after the initial twenty-four hours, you run the risk of serving some prison time.

From the time we parked the skimmer and walked to the airport, I counted seven bodies in various stages of death on the tarmac. Most of them had been carrying sad little suitcases with them, their symbols of hope in this new land, and now the contents of the suitcases blew across the tarmac, shirts and trousers and festive little underthings for the women.

There was a Federation office on the second floor of the airport. McClure burst through the door, and Betsy and I followed in his wake.

We took seats in the outer office while McClure went into a door marked PRIVATE. Almost immediately, somebody, a male, started yelling at him.

The secretary looked at us and smiled.

"That Bjornsen, what a kidder."

"He's not really mad at McClure?" Betsy said.

"Oh, he's really mad all right, but only on the outside."

"I see."

"Inside, he's just like a papa to all his agents. Gruff but loving."

"Gruff but loving." Betsy repeated and winked at me.

Apparently, Bjornsen was tuning up the Gruff knob because now, in addition to yelling at McClure, he was also throwing stuff.

"What kind of stupid bastard would let her get away!"

Something smashed against the wall.

"And what kind of stupid bastard wouldn't have grabbed the kid when he had a chance!"

Something else smashed against the wall.

Each time Bjornsen smashed something against

the wall, the secretary's entire body twitched and continue to twitch for moments after. She had developed, over the years working with gruff but loving Bjornsen, a bad case of shell shock.

"And worst of all, what kind of stupid bastard would bring a couple of low-rent skimmer pilots back with him to help on the investigation."

The secretary looked at us.

"Don't take it personally," she said, looking embarrassed.

"Gruff but loving," Betsy smiled.

This time, Bjornsen didn't settle for smashing something against the wall. He turned something over. Something heavy. A bookcase, maybe.

"On second thought," the secretary said, getting up from behind her desk, "maybe I'll visit the tinkle room."

She left with tears in her eyes and twitching badly.

McClure stayed in there for ten more minutes.

During that time, the secretary never came back.

I didn't blame her.

"Well," I said, "how long's it been since you've thought about your flyboy?"

Betsy looked at me and grinned.

"You know, I don't even remember. I mean, it's been at least half a day or something. I've been too busy thinking about you, Duvall. Have you been thinking about me?"

"Maybe."

She poked me in the ribs.

"You've been thinking about me a lot, haven't you?"

I smiled. "Well, maybe a little."

"Jerk."

"All right, a lot."

This time, she smiled.

Then: "You think Sara'll be at that address?"

I shrugged. "We've got to start somewhere. But she knows that I saw that address scribbled on the back of the article so she's got to assume we'll at least pay a visit there."

"I just hope that Sara lets us take her."

I hadn't told her what McClure had said to me about Sara's plan to use Emily to reposition the warheads, and then to blackmail the Federation.

Now seemed a good time.

"So the strain of doing it could make Emily lose her mind?" she said.

"I'm afraid so. I remember reading about some of the psi students that the Federation was experimenting with. A lot of them ended up in mental institutions the rest of their lives."

"I just don't see how Sara could do that to her own daughter."

"She's a revolutionary," I said, "and for her the revolution comes before everything else. That's why her husband was trying to get Emily back from her. He wanted to protect her. And that's why Sara killed him."

We sat with our private thoughts in the small gray office with the Federation flag on one wall, filing cabinets lined against another wall, and a window view of the airport tarmac filling a third wall.

Far out on the tarmac now, a couple of guards and a couple of dogs were chasing two kids who were probably ten or so. The guards had just killed the parents. Now they wanted to finish off the rest of the family. I tried not to think of my daughter, and how the lynch mob had dragged her from the house.

The kids were a lot more resilient than you might imagine.

They ran hard for another two or three minutes before the dogs finally caught up with them and brought them down.

At least the guards finished them off quickly.

Just a couple of brief bursts from their weapons, and the kids were dead.

One of the guards took a trash bag from his backpack and got to work stuffing the kids inside.

"You think she'd really destroy Los Angeles?" Betsy asked.

"Are you kidding? She'd love it. The more innocent people she can slaughter, the better."

"You make her sound like a monster."

I looked at her and said, "Don't go getting sentimental about her, Betsy. She is a monster."

"Yeah, but she's also Emily's mother. That should count for something."

"She hatched her," I said. "That's about it. Any civilizing influences that Emily's had probably came from her father. Let me remind you of just one thing: Sara doesn't see anything wrong with blowing up hospitals to terrorize the Federation. That's what makes her a monster."

Betsy gave a helpless little shrug.

"I guess her face is what gets me. She's so beautiful, she almost looks like an angel."

"Don't forget that Satan was an angel at one time, too."

Betsy smiled sadly.

"All right, Duvall. You've convinced me. She's a monster." Then, more quietly: "She really is a monster, isn't she?"

The question was rhetorical, but even if I'd wanted to answer, Betsy wouldn't have been able to hear me because just then an alarm went off that sounded as if it were signaling Armageddon.

Bjornsen's door flew back wide and framed in it was McClure.

"They've found Sara Ford at Gate Six! There's a positive scent match! Let's go get her!"

And once again, we were following McClure—

Out the door, down the hall, nearly knocking down Bjornsen's secretary as she emerged from tinkling, and then to an Emergency walkway that McClure had the code to. Then we were traveling forty mph, hurtling toward Gate Six.

Maybe capturing Sara Ford wasn't going to be so difficult after all.

The Federation keeps a database with more than six million names they suspect of being Front sympathizers. If you happen to get detained for any reason, the Federation takes the opportunity to get your fingerprints, your retina ID, your DNA and your scent identification as well. Smells can be as telling as fingerprints and DNA.

Apparently, this was how Sara Ford was discovered, a security guard, who had been given Sara's scent to trace, had found her at one of the far gates trying to get into a skycab.

McClure allowed himself a grin.

"Man, I don't even like to *think* about what that woman could've done if she'd ever gotten her daughter to start playing with those nuclear warheads."

I had to agree with him.

Much as I hated the Federation, I didn't want to see six or seven million innocent people destroyed.

We were nearing Gate Six now.

A crowd ringed the entire gate entrance now.

This was better than holos.

This was the real thing—actual criminals brought to justice—and what bored airport passenger would want to miss out on something like that?

Security people tried to clear them away, but the crowd had decided not to budge.

They had front row tickets and they were damned well going to use them.

McClure forced his way through the crowd— with several people calling him names, and pushing back at him—and Betsy and I followed him.

Airport security, a robot and two human beings had a frightened-looking woman pressed back against the wall. Her hands were up. She looked to be about thirty, scruffy and dirty. If I'd had to guess, I would have pegged her as one of the religious cultists who prey on airport customers.

One of the security techs had some kind of scenting device running up and down the woman's body.

Betsy spotted it before I did.

"That blouse," she said.

Beneath her shabby brown jacket, the woman wore a silk blouse of peach color and stylish design. The same blouse that Sara Ford had been wearing.

"This is her, all right," one of the security techs said to McClure, who had identified himself only moments ago. "This electronic nose is going nuts. The computer identified her as Sara Ford."

"She tricked us," I said to McClure.

"What?" he said, turning to look at me.

I stepped forward.

"Did a very good-looking woman give you this blouse just a while ago?"

The woman being detained looked terrified.

"I never did nothin' wrong, honest," she said around tiny brown stumps of teeth. "I only come out here to preach the Word, you know, about Christ and all."

"Ma'am, please listen to me," I said.

She was so scared she was simply babbling words.

A new scent had been added to the others.

The woman's fear had caused her to wet herself.

She wasn't real easy to stand next to, her being in bad need of a shower and all, but I felt sorry for her.

"Ma'am, listen to me."

She looked at me.

"I'm trying to help you. I want to be your friend. All right?"

Many of the cultists who worked the airport were clinically insane. The vacuous blue gaze of this woman made me wonder if she were sane.

"Ma'am."

"Yes."

"That isn't your blouse, is it?"

"I never stole it."

"Somebody gave it to you, didn't they?"

"I never stole it. Honest, I didn't."

She was getting scared again, tears in her eyes and voice.

"How long ago did she give it to you?"

But she said nothing.

"She tricked us," McClure said, giving up on the woman. "Sara Ford gives this woman her blouse, so that it'll throw our trackers off."

"We follow this woman instead of Sara Ford," I said, "who's long gone by now."

The woman grabbed my sleeve.

"I never stole this. Honest, I didn't."

She was obviously certain she was going to get arrested.

"Everything'll be all right, ma'am."

I took her hand and patted it.

She smiled at me with her heartbreakingly bad teeth.

"The mister, he always done that to me, patted me like that," she said, nodding to where my hand covered hers. "When he was alive and all."

"One of the security techs will take you into the restroom and you can take off that blouse."

"I ain't gonna get in any trouble?"

"No," I said. "No trouble."

"They won't arrest me?"

"No, ma'am."

"They arrested Earle that time, and I never seen him again."

"You'll be fine, ma'am, you really will."

She'd started crying again.

"What do you think they done with Earle, mister? Huh? What do you think they done with him?"

2

The best way to see L.A. is from a skycar. You don't get the smell of the various ghettos that way, nor do you hear the constant gunfire, gang-to-gang, cops-to-gang. If you watch the freeways carefully, though, you do see the ambulances, red cherries flashing every mile or so along the unending stretches of L.A. expressway. Up in the hills and along certain parts of the ocean is where you find the L.A. life of fable: the mansions, the cliffside dwellings, the swimming pools. Here, you also find security choppers crisscrossing the air space over these fabled areas, choppers that are in constant contact with security forces on the ground. Basically, it's more a military than a police operation. Not only are the houses and the parties fabled out here, so are the thieves, some of whom have attacked estates with tanks and planes.

"You picking up anything?" McClure said.

I'd told him about the psi contact I'd had with Emily.

"You make me sound like a radio."

"Thought we might get lucky."

"I just wish we knew she was all right," Betsy said.

"Well, we know that Sara will take good care of her until the work is done," McClure said. "After that, who knows?"

The address on the back of Sara's article belonged to a sprawling neighborhood that completely encircled a small ghetto area. The people who lived here had enough money to afford two security choppers. Up in the hills, where the real money was, you saw ten security choppers at a time.

"Down there," McClure said to the pilot.

The pilot nodded and started his descent.

The houses and streets looked a lot better from the air than they did on the ground.

A lot of the homes were in bad need of repair, and the streets were littered with all kinds of junked cars that looked to be in agony, like rusted metal beasts breathing their last.

We set down in an alley a few houses away from the address we wanted.

"Wait here," McClure told the pilot.

The three of us scrambled out of the chopper, drew our weapons, and started for the house where we hoped to find Emily and Sara Ford.

The house was an ancient two-story frame with a screened-in back porch and a full-length front porch. The paint was suffering from leprosy; most of the windows had been smashed out, and cardboard backing put up behind them.

We spent a few minutes walking around the exterior of the house, trying to decide the best way in.

Sara Ford wouldn't have any difficulty, physically or ethically, with killing us in our tracks.

"I get the feeling that somebody's watching us," Betsy said.

"Yeah," I said, "so do I."

I scanned the smashed windows, looking for eyes peeking out. I didn't see any.

"Back door," McClure said. "I think that's our best bet."

We walked up the three steps to the screened-in porch. The rusty hinges squawked like a parrot when we opened the door. The porch was packed up with shabby furniture left over from many bygone eras. If I got any closer, the dust in all the stuffing would send my sinuses into chaos.

McClure was at the inside back door, his hand ready to seize the knob.

"Ready?" he said.

"Ready," I said.

Betsy nodded.

McClure tried the knob.

Locked.

He pointed his stunner at it and hit it with some energy.

The knob sheared away, the air smelling of burning metal.

He eased the door open with his foot.

We followed him inside.

We stood in a kitchen that was a health hazard. Unwashed dishes from many, many meals overflowed the sink and took up most of the counter space. A rat the size of a kitten sat atop one pile of dishes, glaring at us with complete confidence. He seemed absolutely sure that we were the intruders, not he.

McClure nodded to the house beyond the kitchen.

We walked on tiptoes.

There was a short, dark hallway with a closet off to the right. I tried the door. The suffocating scent of mothballs filled my nostrils. A few shabby coats hung in the closet. Otherwise, it was empty.

The living room was surprisingly civilized. A large brick fireplace lent a warmth to a room with built-in bookcases along the west wall and French doors on the north wall. The furniture, while old and dusty, was a couch and chair of good dark leather.

The shell casings on the floor spoiled the civilized air somewhat, as did the splash of blood on the east wall. It looked as if somebody had bled a great deal and then been slammed into the wall.

McClure cursed.

If anybody was here, they were in the basement or upstairs.

He nodded silently to the short staircase leading to the next floor.

He led us up the stairs. Tiptoes again. Weapons drawn.

At midpoint, we heard something and stopped cold.

A few moments later, a calico cat flounced across the hall at the top of the stairs, carrying a freshly killed mouse in her teeth.

She walked with a great deal of pride and satisfaction in her gait. She favored us with a fleeting and somewhat disdainful look, and then kept on walking.

We crept up the stairs.

The second floor was small and crowded and shadowy. The walls and floors made loud settling noises.

There were six small rooms. We each took two.

My two included a sewing room and a bathroom. Nothing to be seen. The bathroom was almost as scuzzy as the kitchen, which was no small accomplishment.

I was just backing out of the john, the stench starting to get serious in my nostrils, when I heard McClure say, "Shit."

I walked quickly down the hall.

McClure was in a bedroom. A guy was on the bed, flat on his back. His stomach had been hit with a laser. It boiled and bubbled, raw. Stomachs weren't supposed to do that. He was alive, but not in any meaningful way. His sorrowful blue eyes were open, watching us. He was trying to be brave, or at least accepting of his inevitable death, but it wasn't working out so well. He looked scared.

We walked over to the head of the bed.

The guy, who had a face covered with tattoos, continued to watch us as he moaned and sometimes sobbed.

"Where's Sara Ford?" I said.

I could see the recognition in his eyes.

The guy wore a white shirt and dark trousers. He stank pretty bad.

"Where's Sara Ford?"

"That bitch."

I couldn't argue with him about that.

McClure didn't have my patience.

He put the muzzle of his weapon to the man's forehead.

"Where's Sara Ford?" McClure said.

The guy smiled.

"Go ahead, man. You'd be doing me a favor."

There was no way you were going to threaten this guy with death. He was already well on his way.

I said, in a soft voice, "You know her daughter?"

"Emily?"

"Yeah."

"She's a sweetie."

"She won't be when Sara gets done with her. She'll be dead or in a mental hospital the rest of her life."

The guy stared at me a minute.

"You know about the warheads, huh?" Then he grimaced and grabbed for his stomach. His hands were bloody red from touching his open wound.

"Yeah," I said. "I do."

"I didn't want her to do it. That's why she killed me. Said I was a chickenshit and I didn't really care about the revolution at all." He shook his sweaty head. "I just couldn't see killing all those kids. I mean, I hate the Federation as much as she does but I still don't want to kill all the kids in L.A."

"It wouldn't faze Sara," I said.

He smiled. Sweat beaded his forehead. His eyes still looked scared. "You must know her pretty well."

"Know the type," I said.

"Where is she now?" McClure snapped.

We were playing good cop, bad cop with the dying guy.

"You have to shout, man?" the guy said.

"We're in a hurry, asshole," McClure said. "Thanks to your friends, the whole city of L.A. is in danger."

I went into the bathroom and soaked a towel in cold water and came back in and put it on the dying guy's forehead.

"Thanks, man."

I nodded.

"You have any idea where she might be?"

"I'm not sure."

"She give you any hint?"

He thought a moment.

"Not today, she didn't. She wasn't talking to me too much today. I was supposed to have some money for her, but I didn't get it."

"Why'd she need money?" I said.

"Pay off some old fart who used to work for the psi school the Federation ran up in the hills. That's where Emily went to classes for a long time. That's where they learned how high her psi potential was."

"Why'd they want to pay off the old guy?"

"He used to be Emily's favorite teacher. Sara figured that if she could get him to help Emily move the missiles telepathically—well, maybe Emily would feel better about having Dr. Wenright there with her."

"Where's the school?" I said.

"I know where it is," McClure said.

Just then the guy screamed.

That's the trouble with getting it in the stomach that way. There may be slower and more painful ways to die, but I haven't heard of them.

"You ask him to leave?" the guy said.

"McClure, you mean?"

"Yeah, him."

I nodded to the door. McClure didn't look happy, but he went.

"We have to get going," he said, as he walked out the door.

When we were alone, the guy said, "Finish me off, will you?"

"You sure?"

He smiled.

"I'm sure unless you've got a couple of miracles on hand."

He was right. Even if we got him to a hospital, it was too late to save him.

"Please," he said. "Now."

I pointed the weapon right at his heart.

"I appreciate this, man, I really do."

I killed him quick.

In the chopper, when Betsy and the pilot were waiting for us, McClure said, "I didn't like that guy."

"Oh, yeah?" I said. "Well, he didn't like you either."

The pilot took us up and away.

3

A religious cult had heard about the experiments being conducted in the Federation psi school, and had decided to destroy the building since its existence obviously pissed off Jesus. They were not what you'd call munitions experts, these fine religious folk, so it took them three different tries to reduce three wings of the school to rubble. They never did get the center of the building, where most of the heaviest psi experiments were staged. But they did succeed in closing the whole operation down. Jesus was no doubt pleased. At least *their* version of Jesus, who bore no resemblance to the one I'd read about, the one of tolerance and forgiveness and peace.

From a skycar, the tumbled down parts of the deserted school looked as if a tornado had torn apart the most extreme edges, which were now piles of brick and ash. And while the center section was still standing, no windows remained intact, there was a massive hole in the roof, and much of the facade showed gouging from where the explosion had hurled bricks at it. The grass was overgrown; wild dogs roamed the rubble.

The only sign of life was a skycar parked near the back of the building. It looked impossibly new and shiny. No doubt Sara had rented it.

"We'd better land about a quarter of a mile away and walk back," I said. "Otherwise, they'll see us for sure."

"Good idea," McClure said.

"I just hope they haven't started yet," Betsy said.

She was obviously thinking about Emily.

There was a burned-out area near a copse of trees that made a perfect landing spot.

We set off walking right away.

"You know anything about this teacher of hers?" I said to McClure as we walked.

"Not much. His name is Wenright and he's a real eccentric. Or was. For a long time we suspected he might be a double agent." McClure smiled coldly at me. "He wasn't. He was just like you. He hated both sides."

"But he worked for the Federation anyway?" Betsy inquired.

"Science," McClure said. "That's all he was interested in. He believed that once the human species realized its psi potential, we'd be a lot happier as a species."

"You ever think that maybe he was right?" I said.

McClure shook his head.

"For a smart guy, you're awfully naive, Duvall.

The Federation would love to sit down and talk with the Zoners, but as long as Sara Ford and her people keep blowing up hospitals and schools— no way."

"You could always stop lynching people to show your good faith," I said.

Betsy, who knew about my wife and daughter, slid her arm through mine and hugged me.

"We're doing the Undesirables a favor," McClure said. "Why should they hide out forever in fear? It's easier to just get it done with."

Now he was the McClure I'd originally met, the one I hated just as much as I hated Sara Ford, the true believer who felt that anything he did was justified in the name of the cause.

Betsy gave another little tug on my arm to keep me from saying anything to him.

It was just as well. In the face of that kind of bigotry, there's nothing to say anyway.

The closer we got to the school, the deeper the grass and weeds became.

We circled wide, coming out at the back door of the place.

We spent a few minutes searching the windows for any evidence of human eyes watching us.

Sara would have no problem with shooting us on sight.

But no eyes appeared in the windows.

We crept up to the door, weapons drawn.

The door was open and we went inside.

It's a funny thing about schools. Even after they've been deserted a long time, even after they've been corrupted by dust, dirt, and various kinds of animal feces, they still smell like schools, that high faint scent of floor wax and chalk dust. Despite all the overheads and all the computers, some teachers still preferred chalk and old-fashioned blackboards.

I got sentimental standing there in the hall. I was a fourteen-year-old again and it was the first day of ninth grade and I was falling in love about once every five minutes, as all these gorgeous tenth and eleventh and twelfth grade girls swirled by me.

Then I stepped in some doggy doo, and my sentimental dream disappeared.

"I'll be right back," I said.

"Scrape it off your boot?" Betsy asked.

I nodded.

I was back in two minutes. I'd not only cleaned the boot off on the grass, I'd found an old can filled with rainwater. I dipped my boot in and cleaned it off really good.

"That feels better," I said to Betsy.

McClure just looked annoyed that I'd held things up.

"Let's fan out and start looking for them," McClure said, much as he had when we'd reached the second floor of the house we'd just been in.

We fanned out.

There were three levels. I took the basement.

As soon as I reached the bottom of the stairs, I found myself in a long, dark tunnel. There were no lights to turn on. I had a small flashlight and used that.

The bodies sort of bothered me at first, but by the time I got to the other end of the tunnel, I was used to them.

People who didn't want others to know they had the Plague oftentimes hid out so that they could die peacefully. In the early years of the Plague, the good old teenage lynch mobs hanged anybody they even remotely suspected of having the Plague.

So a lot of people went off and hid somewhere the way animals did when their time came to die.

I counted eleven bodies, now mostly skeletons, lining the corridor walls down here.

I shone my light in the classrooms but found nothing more than dusty desks and cobwebbed computer terminals.

Rats still sniffed around the corpses. Though they'd obviously stripped the dead people of all meat, the rats just had to make sure that there wasn't anything left. Like human beings, they could never quite accept the fact that their luck had run out.

When I reached the other end of the corridor, I walked up the steps and then heard the voices.

They came from the darkness of the basement. But from where? I'd checked every room.

I worked my way back down the steps, listening carefully to the darkness.

Voices, faint but unmistakable.

I trained my light along the wall, looking for some kind of opening in the wall. None.

I walked the entire length of the corridor again, and still found nothing.

But the voices remained, faint, almost dreamlike.

I went back down the corridor once more, the way I'd just come. As I neared the end of it, the voices grew louder momentarily. I recognized Sara's voice. She snapped her words out angrily.

I'd checked the janitor's closet out earlier but had found nothing. Now I decided to try it again.

The closet smelled of furniture polish and disinfectant, a sweet-sour aroma that made my eyes water.

I played my light over all the walls of the cramped closet.

At first, everything looked normal. Brooms, mops, buckets—all the things you'd expect to find in such a closet.

Then I moved the cases of toilet paper that were stacked to the ceiling.

A tiny line ran from the ceiling to the floor. I pressed my ear to this section of the wall. The voices came clearer now.

They were coming up from below.

Obviously there was a subbasement.

I leaned against the hairline indentation in the wall. I pushed at the top, in the middle, along the bottom. Nothing happened.

The voices were louder. Sara and the old professor were arguing about something.

I tried running my fingers along the hairline from top to bottom. Still nothing. The wall remained unmovable.

I was getting down on my knees to examine the floor when my foot banged against a piece of wood trim running along the bottom of the wall.

The wall started opening quickly and quietly.

I thought of going back to get Betsy and McClure but then I realized that this might be my only chance to get to the subbasement.

As I descended the steps that wound deep into a shadowy subterranean world, the temperature must have dropped ten degrees.

Light spilled from a room off the bottom of the stairs.

Now the voices were very clear.

"But, Sara, if you make her do this—she might never recover. You have to understand the consequences of this."

The voice was old, male, and very intelligent. It was also wearily sad. Being around Sara Ford's kind of hatred for any length of time could do that to you.

"Finish working with her, Doctor, or I'll kill you right on the spot."

I moved up to the doorway as quietly as possible and then peeked inside.

In the center of a large, empty room was a tall, wide dais.

Emily sat in a chair in the center of the dais. On

her left was her mother, on her right was the doctor.

The doctor said, "She doesn't want to do this, Sara. Can't you see that's why it's not working? She doesn't want to do it, and there's no way we can force her."

Sara stepped closer to Emily.

She slapped the girl with extraordinary, echoing force. Emily's head snapped back.

"I'm tired of this, Emily," Sara said. "You know what you're supposed to do, and I want you to do it right now."

"I don't want to hurt all these people," Emily answered. "The doctor told me what will happen if I move all those missiles."

"The doctor should learn to keep his damned mouth shut," Sara said.

Doctor Wenright shook his head. He was a very old man with a baby-pink scalp, arthritically gnarled hands and a threadbare cardigan sweater and even more threadbare corduroy pants.

"Now, Emily," Sara cajoled, her voice calmer now. "I want you to concentrate. I know you can do this. Even Wenright admits you can do it. So all we need is for you to concentrate. Do you understand?"

"But, Mama—"

Sara decided to play the put-upon mother rather than the angry despot.

"Do you have any idea how much it takes for me to protect you from bad people, Emily?"

"Well—"

"Well, do you?"

"I know you protect me, Mama, but—"

"And do you have any idea how many Undesirables the Federation has killed over the years?"

"I know they're bad people, Mama."

"They're terrible people, Emily. You're not old enough yet to understand how terrible."

"But Dr. Wenright said we'd kill innocent girls and boys—"

"We won't kill them, Emily. That's the beauty of this. We'll simply bluff them. We'll have them release all our prisoners they're holding, and we'll make them pay billions and billions of dollars in reparations for how they've treated us over the years."

"Don't listen to her, Emily," Wenright said. "The first thing she'll do is destroy Los Angeles to prove how serious she is. That's when she'll negotiate—after the city has been destroyed. Don't listen to her."

"Just stay right where you are," I said, coming through the door.

Sara and Wenright had been so absorbed in Emily that they didn't see me until it was too late.

"Put the gun down on the dais, Sara," I said.

"You bastard," she said. "You'll regret this. I promise you."

Despite her angry speech, she set her stunner down on the dais.

"Now come down from there, hands over your head."

"I always knew you were a double agent, you asshole," Sara said.

"You know better than that, Sara. I just don't want to see millions of innocent people die." Then: "Did she hurt you, Emily?"

"She just slapped me is all," Emily replied softly. Then: "Is Betsy with you?"

At the mention of Betsy, Sara rolled her eyes. She was at least maternal enough to know that her little girl preferred Betsy as her friend and confidante.

"She's upstairs," I said. "I left the passage open for her. She'll probably be down here very soon."

I suppose I was too concerned about Emily, that's why I didn't notice what Sara did suddenly.

One moment, Dr. Wenright had been standing next to Sara, the next she was getting him in a choke hold, with a long, gleaming knife held to his throat. I should have figured that Sara would be armed with more than a stunner.

"I'll cut his throat," she said.

"I know you will."

"Come over here and put your weapon on the dais."

"If you make her do this, she'll go insane," I said. "Or maybe even die."

"She's old enough to understand that sometimes you have to make sacrifices. Now put your gun over here."

Dr Wenright looked as confused as he did scared, as if he hadn't been able to absorb the significance yet of what had happened. He looked old and depleted.

I went over and put my gun on the dais.

"Push it over here."

I pushed it to her.

"Why was there this subbasement?" I asked.

"When you roll that door closed, you're completely cut off from all outside stimuli in here. The walls were baffled in such a way that you couldn't even hear an explosion in the hallway. Dr. Wenright worked with his best students in here. He got them to do all sorts of things for the Federation, didn't you, Doctor?"

At the mention of the Federation, her voice turned nasty again. The edge of her knife drew a little blood from Wenright's throat. He yelped in shock and pain.

"Emily," Sara said, "I want you to listen to me very carefully. All right?"

"I don't want you to hurt Dr. Wenright."

"Good. Then you know what's going on here. If you don't move those missiles, I'm going to kill him right here and right now. You know I will, don't you?"

Emily's face was a composite of fear and grief. She was silent for a moment, then: "Yes, Mother. I'll do what you want."

"But, Emily—"

As soon as Wenright started to speak, Sara drew the knife across his throat again. She didn't cut him much, just enough to terrorize him for a few more minutes. Sara was a past master at the low and subtle art of terrorizing people.

"Go ahead, Emily. Now."

Emily took a deep breath, drew herself up in her chair, shoulders back, head held high.

"Remember the photographs I showed you of the missile sites, Emily," Sara said. "Are you thinking of them?"

"Yes."

"Good. Now picture the aerial overviews I showed you—the land around the missile sites. Are you picturing that, too?"

"Yes."

"Concentrate on the missiles first."

Emily's face tightened, her eyes squeezing shut.

"Do you understand the direction north?"

"Yes."

"Turn the missiles north."

Emily's face grew even tighter. Her breathing started to sound labored now. Sweat shone on her forehead.

Long moments went by in the big, empty room, the only sound being Emily's breathing, which was now coming in gasps.

I could almost feel the missiles being turned in a northerly direction. I had no doubts about Emily's powers.

I also had no doubts about what would happen before this day was over: Sara meant to destroy Los Angeles.

Whimpers could now be heard in Emily's

throat. And suddenly, her upper body began to spasm and twitch.

"Look what you're doing to her," Wenright said. "She's your own daughter."

Sara had only one comment. She sliced a little more from Wenright's neck.

"Keep going, Emily," Sara said, speaking in a voice so soothing, it didn't sound like her.

I watched the first few moments of it, but I wasn't able to tell what was going on.

The knife disappeared and her stunner filled her hand. She didn't loosen her grip at all on Wenright.

I heard shouts from the back of the room but by the time I turned around to see who'd called out, I saw Betsy, framed in the doorway, drop to her knees. Sara had shot her just below the neck.

Sara squeezed off another shot quickly and McClure's stunner went flying from his hand.

"Bring her up here," Sara told McClure, nodding at Betsy, who lay unmoving on the floor.

McClure didn't have much choice but to obey.

4

It was another twenty minutes before Emily started screaming, and in the meantime, Sara did her best to keep all of us in one place so she could keep us within easy trigger distance.

She told us to sit on the floor against the nearest wall. There was a small table to the right of us, the only other piece of furniture in the room.

I got Betsy propped up between McClure and myself and then I started looking at her wound.

The laser had cut open a small hole that was ringed with singed and puckered flesh. Laser poisoning is pretty common with this sort of wound—the poison kills more people than most wounds—so I spent a few minutes trying to gauge her body temperature.

Most of the time, she was unconscious, propped against the wall, her head leaning against my shoulder.

In that twenty-minute period, I checked her temperature three times. She felt marginally warmer each time I touched her.

McClure couldn't sit still. His fear of Los Angeles being nuked translated to a bad case of the jitters. It was difficult to pace sitting down, but he seemed to be doing just that, his hands and feet in constant motion, apparently in time to some rhythmic music only he could hear.

Wenright cursed when the blood started dripping from Emily's ear and pooling on her shoulder.

"I told you, I told you," he said angrily to Sara.

"It doesn't mean anything," Sara said, "it's just a little blood."

" 'Just a little blood.' " Wenwright mocked her.

His gnarled body managed to bend over and he took Emily's hands gently.

Her entire body was rocking.

The blood continued to drip from her ear, only faster now.

A cry was strangled in her throat.

Watching her, I felt as if I was observing an engine that was just whining to full capacity, and would soon explode if it continued to race this way.

Emily screamed so loudly that even her mother took note, looking a little intimidated by her daughter at this moment.

Sara demanded complete control of every situation.

She clearly sensed that she was losing control of this one.

Emily sat there, rocking from side to side,

almost slipping out of her chair at a couple of points.

Blood sprayed from her other ear now.

"My God!" Wenright said.

Then, to Sara: "I want you to stop her! She's gone far enough now!"

Sara leaned in and put a hand on Emily's shoulder.

But it did no good.

Emily was shaking so hard that her mother's hand was pitched off.

I thought of the engine again. The engine was soon to be completely out of control.

Another scream.

And that was when I first heard the ceiling begin to tear apart.

Several years earlier I'd been in Los Angeles during a minor earthquake.

This feeling was similar. The floor began to move like an escalator that went side to side instead of up and down.

"Stop, Emily! Stop now!"

Even though Wenright was shouting, he could scarcely be heard.

The entire building was beginning to fold in on itself, the walls caving in, the ceiling coming down in huge dusty chunks.

Wenright cried out again, but between the crumbling building and Emily's strange wailing, he could scarcely be heard.

Wenright grabbed Emily and tried to cover her with his body, to protect her from falling debris.

Sara pushed him aside, knocking him down, directly into the path of a large chunk of ceiling.

I had to look away as the chunk slammed old Wenright to the floor and then smashed him down. Another piece of debris caught Sara. She cried out and put her hands—as if pleading—up in the air. But the debris came down anyway, crushing her.

Then there was no time to look or even cry out. I reached over and grabbed the small table by one of its legs and pulled it over our heads to protect us. I grabbed McClure and yanked him under the table.

Then the rest of the ceiling gave way.

I can't really tell you what happened over the next five minutes or so.

The building came apart is, I suppose, the simplest way to say it.

I hugged Betsy to me, as careful of her wound as I could be, trying to keep her head beneath the protection of not only the tabletop but my arm as well.

I felt as if I were in a volcano at this point, dust from the crumbling building as heavy as fog, a rumbling in the ground itself as various parts of the floor cracked throughout the building.

Then, in the awful silence that followed, I heard Emily's voice say, clearly and quietly, "I'd appreciate it if somebody could help me. I'm stuck under this big piece of concrete."

5

Six days after we rescued Emily, Mae walked into Federation headquarters in New York and set down in front of the Federation President a list of twelve demands.

He was ready with his own list. He had eight demands.

They didn't like each other, Mae and the Pres, and they didn't trust each other, but they did sit there for four hours and call each other names, and even made a few concessions per their lists of demands.

The Pres made four concessions and Mae made two. It was a start, anyway.

Mae saved the best news for last.

Over the past week, the doctors who'd been experimenting with Plague patients in the Zone had learned that a special antibody only found in Undesirables could actually cure the worst of the Plague symptoms. That's why the isolated patient at Mae's hospital had been able to shed the Plague.

So here, as Mae put it, was the deal. If the

Federation continued to talk seriously about abolishing the Zone and becoming one nation again, then a) Mae would make all the Zone scientists available to the Federation and, b) if the Federation refused to negotiate in good faith, even given the cure for the Plague, then Emily who could still manipulate the missiles pointed at Los Angeles, was going to blow the hell out of everything.

The Pres decided it would probably be a good idea to negotiate in good faith. There was nothing like some nuclear warheads aimed at a major city to get your attention.

Mae told me all this later on over a communicator. She also told me that she was wearing a khaki uniform pretty much like the one General Douglas MacArthur used to wear. "It's pretty cool," she laughed.

Mae was now the Pres of the Zone, and would likely be an important political figure when integration finally took place.

As for McClure . . . well, he became the de facto hero of the whole thing. If he hadn't tracked down this guy named Duvall, then none of this would have happened. The Pres gave him a parade and he started making the rounds of all the holo talkies, his heroism growing a little bit each time he referred to it, and he dumped his old wife and got himself a beautiful, if somewhat vacuous, new babe, as well as a skycar that had glowing bat wings instead of fenders, and a hologram of McClure on each door. He was appropriately dressed in a WWI flying cap with a long white scarf flowing over his shoulder.

As for Betsy, Emily, and I . . . Well, no offense, but don't ask. It's been a year since Mae and Pres started fashioning our brave new world. Sometimes Emily gets sentimental about her mother, and cries. Funny how you can love somebody who never much loved you.

Let's just say that we live somewhere in the continental United States and that we've all had our physical appearance surgically altered right down to our retina prints. Not even the best agents of the Federation can find us. And never will.

We're close to forests and animals and clear, tumbling mountain water. We're close to sky and mountain and stars. We have a wonderful life. Betsy's even managed to forget all about the pilot who broke her heart.

But best of all, we've been able to help bring the Federation and the Zone together.

Emily has been able to skew the warheads in such a way that only she can manipulate them without blowing them up.

This has a way of focusing the attention of Mae and the others at the negotiating table.

And the same with the Plague. They've pretty much cured it now, and in another couple of years there'll be no traces left at all.

Emily's even made peace with her mother.

I built a small stone marker with her mother's

name on it. I built it high on a hill where the wind comes crisp and clean and where the music of jays soothes even the most frazzled nerves.

Betsy and I stand on the porch and watch her sometimes, the slender blind girl making her way up the hill to the grave marker.

The other day she came down from the hill and threw herself into Betsy's arms and said, "I just had a great experience up there." It was odd, the way she was crying. She sounded happy and sad at the same time.

"What happened?" Betsy said.

Emily slid her arms around both of us and brought us close together.

"I told her I forgave her, and that I loved her," Emily said. "And I told her about my new mom and dad," she added. Then she held us a little tighter.

And you know what?

Right then, I felt like crying, too. I really did.

DANIEL RANSOM

☐ **ZONE SOLDIERS** UE2737—$5.99

The accidental release of a deadly virus violently transformed the United States into two armed camps: the "Normals" of the Federation and the mutant "Undesirables" in the Zone. Now, sixty-three years after the cataclysm, a terrorist mutant rights organization known as the Front is striking back at the Federation in a winner-take-all bid that will decide the future of all humanity!

☐ **THE FUGITIVE STARS** UE2625—$4.99

The tail of the comet held more than just harmless space dust. It also contained the seeds of an alien invasion. The alien lifeforms spread throughout the population with amazing speed, taking over the bodies of their human hosts and using them to reach all the way to the Oval Office. Only one man could sense what was happening, but could he prove it before it was too late?

Eluki bes Shahar

THE HELLFLOWER SERIES

☐ **HELLFLOWER (Book 1)** UE2475—$3.99

Butterfly St. Cyr had a well-deserved reputation as an honest and dependable smuggler. But when she and her partner, a highly illegal artificial intelligence, rescued Tiggy, the son and heir to one of the most powerful of the hellflower mercenary leaders, it looked like they'd finally taken on more than they could handle. For his father's enemies had sworn to see that Tiggy and Butterfly never reached his home planet alive. . . .

☐ **DARKTRADERS (Book 2)** UE2507—$4.50

With her former partner Paladin—the death-to-possess Old Federation artificial intelligence—gone off on a private mission, Butterfly didn't have anybody to back her up when Tiggy's enemies decided to give the word "ambush" a whole new and all-too-final meaning.

☐ **ARCHANGEL BLUES (Book 3)** UE2543—$4.50

Darktrader Butterfly St. Cyr and her partner Tiggy seek to complete the mission they started in DARKTRADERS, to find and destroy the real Archangel, Governor-General of the Empire, the being who is determined to wield A.I. powers to become the master of the entire universe.

More Top-Flight Science Fiction and Fantasy from
C.J. CHERRYH

SCIENCE FICTION
☐ FOREIGNER (hardcover)   UE2590—$20.00
☐ FOREIGNER   UE2637—$5.99
☐ INVADER (hardcover)   UE2638—$19.95
☐ INVADER   UE2687—$5.99
☐ INHERITOR (hardcover)   UE2689—$21.95

THE MORGAINE CYCLE
☐ GATE OF IVREL (BOOK 1)   UE2321—$4.50
☐ WELLS OF SHIUAN (BOOK 2)   UE2322—$4.50
☐ FIRES OF AZEROTH (BOOK 3)   UE2323—$4.50
☐ EXILE'S GATE (BOOK 4)   UE2254—$5.50

FANTASY
The Ealdwood Novels
☐ THE DREAMSTONE   UE2013—$2.95
☐ THE TREE OF SWORDS AND JEWELS

                                              UE1850—$2.95

Kate Elliott

The Novels of the Jaran:

☐ **JARAN: Book 1** UE2513—$5.99
Here is the poignant and powerful story of a young woman's coming of age on an alien world, where she is both player and pawn in an interstellar game of intrigue and politics.

☐ **AN EARTHLY CROWN: Book 2** UE2546—$5.99
The jaran people, led by Ilya Bakhtiian and his Earth-born wife Tess, are sweeping across the planet Rhui on a campaign of conquest. But even more important is the battle between Ilya and Duke Charles, Tess' brother, who is ruler of this sector of space.

☐ **HIS CONQUERING SWORD: Book 3** UE2551—$5.99
Even as Jaran warlord Ilya continues the conquest of his world, he faces a far more dangerous power struggle with his wife's brother, leader of an underground human rebellion against the alien empire.

☐ **THE LAW OF BECOMING: Book 4** UE2580—$5.99
On Rhui, Ilya's son inadvertently becomes the catalyst for what could prove a major shift of power. And in the heart of the empire, the most surprising move of all was about to occur as the Emperor added an unexpected new player to the Game of Princes . . .

Cheryl J. Franklin

KAREN HABER

☐ **WOMAN WITHOUT A SHADOW**   UE2627—$4.99
A fugitive in a galaxy wary of anyone with mind powers and
all too willing to turn her in for the bounty on her head, Kayla,
a gifted telepath, is about to be caught in a struggle between
two deadly forces who will stop at nothing for total victory.

☐ **THE WAR MINSTRELS**   UE2669—$4.99
Kayla has been on the run since she used her mind powers
to strike out at another human. And in a solar system where
her only allies are pirates and aliens, and her enemies have
sworn to see her enslaved or dead, how long can even a triple
empath such as herself hope to survive?

☐ **SISTER BLOOD**   UE2708—$5.99
The rebel forces of the War Minstrels had struck a crucial blow
at the heart of Yates Keller's empire, only to discover that the
capital was a city in ruins, sucked dry to fuel Keller's greed.
But even as she chased Keller to a distant star system, trouble
was brewing among the War Minstrels themselves. And if
Kayla didn't finish her mission soon, a successful revolution
might become the deadliest kind of anarchy.